The Daring Duke's Little Impulse

Darling Duchesses, Book 2

Alyssa Bailey

Love the inside scoop? Sign up for my Newsletter with special offers and bonus content.
https://www.alyssabaileyromance.com

Also by Alyssa Bailey

Darling Duchesses
The Daring Dukes Little Impulse

Watch for more at alyssabailey.com.

The Daring Duke's Little Impulse

He wanted to wrap her in cotton wool, gaze upon her loveliness, then listen to her sassy mouth so he could spank her, cuddle her, make love to her and put her back safely in the cotton wool.

Sarah's loving benefactor is dead, the solicitor will sell her home, her only friends in the world are moving, and the man she thought she would one day marry has stopped responding to her. Determined to be the mistress of her own destiny, with or without a man, would be nearly impossible. Her lord, who would be a duke, has stopped corresponding with her. What was to become of her? Time to make her own way, even if she felt woefully unprepared. Needs must.

Richard relished the enormous responsibilities and good business prowess that earned him the nickname the Daring Duke. He set his eye on a sassy untitled young lady that he was sure was receptive to him, but her benefactor, a man Richard respects, thought her too young. Between distance and family deaths, he has not seen Sarah in several years and has no response to his request to ask for her hand. The Daring Duke doesn't give up easily, but what is he to do? Storm the castle?

Series Description

Spice, Sass and Love

Being a Duke can be trying when you have an estate to run and an obligation to keep but for these dukes, it is even harder to find the right duchess when you have strict guidelines. There are no sedate ladies that draw their attention, no perfectly titled misses of interest. These dukes require spice, sass, and love. And they won't stop until they claim the woman they choose.

Cover Design by Joe Dugdale
Editor: Mary Beth Renn
Manufactured in the United States.

The Daring Duke's Little Impulse
Prologue Time to Begin

Lord Horace Henderson was dead. What was she supposed to do now? When eleven-year-old Sarah Elizabeth Morgan's mother died, she had been Lord and Lady Henderson's housekeeper for nearly twenty years. Sadie never knew her father, and her mother never spoke of him except to say he didn't know what he was missing in the sweet daughter they had created. Sadie accepted that to mean he didn't have time for them because her mother was the kindest person Sadie knew. If it weren't for Mr. Arnold and Lord Henderson, she would think all men were selfish.

Before Mrs. Morgan passed from this earth, she made the staff agree to finish raising her daughter. Mr. Arnold was the butler, and Mrs. Arnold was the second in charge. Then Mrs. A took over the housekeeper's job, and the couple had taken her on as their own by mutual consent. So had Lord and Lady Henderson.

Now, at nearly twenty-one, she had spent every day of her life living in the Henderson home, first as her ladyship's maid and later her companion, then Lord Henderson's dedicated companion. And always under the protective wing of Lord Henderson, who was fair and strict. Not everyone agreed, but no one defied their employer more than once. Not even Sadie.

Of course, the old viscount had his footman, and his valet, but he called Sadie his "Miss Fetcher," and she had always loved that. Her ladyship wasn't always best pleased with his manners, and she complained he was not conducting himself the way a viscount should. He would call into the hall with a crisp, decisive tone, or ring for his little Miss Fetcher, and Sadie would come quickly to his side, eager to do his bidding. As she grew, she wasn't as eager to respond at their every call, but never failed to do so, for she loved the couple as much as she loved the Arnolds.

Lady Henderson was not amused. "You aren't calling a dog, my dear. It isn't seemly. Please use her name."

Her husband would give her a raised eyebrow, and she would end with a flutter of her hands and murmur, "I'm only looking out for her understanding of etiquette."

He would pat his wife's hand and say, "The girl will be fine."

And indeed, she was. Sadie knew precisely what to say, in what company, and protocol was something that at least made sense, even if she thought it su-perfluous.

Lord and Lady Henderson never had children, and Lady Clarise Hender-son treated Sadie as though she were hers, although they never left the house to-gether. It was as though Lady Clarise wanted to believe she had a child but did not want to discuss it with anyone outside of her home. Mrs. Arthur wondered if it was because the reality that Sadie, whom she always called Sarah, wasn't her child would have opened old wounds.

Sadie understood that Lady Clarise likely spent more time with her than she would have her own child, so it was a bit of a muddle in the beginning. There were no nannies or governesses for Sadie, but there were plenty of life lessons and indulgences. They found a rhythm in the house, and while Sadie was not seen as their child to the world, anyone who frequented the place knew the truth about it.

Learning was something Sadie did naturally, but she didn't always enjoy the exercise. Lady Henderson gave Sadie lessons on being a young lady that, at first, she resented. Later, Sadie was grateful. That good lady instructed all of Sadie's lady lessons as Mrs. Arnold called them and was exacting in her expectations. Lady Clarise was a lonely woman, but since Sadie was very attentive, she en-joyed the company. No one would have wished Sadie to lose her mother at such a young age, but if it had to be, it worked out well for everyone.

"I love Lord Henderson, but you, Sarah, give me a reason to rise from my bed each day."

It saddened Sadie that her ladyship often felt low, but she took comfort that she was the reason Lady Clarise wasn't too melancholy.

The first genuine encounter with a young man who spoke to her was when she discovered that Lord Griffin, the man Lord Henderson once described as the lord who would be a duke, demonstrated that he watched her with a discerning eye. He didn't hide the fact, either, and that was titillating and disconcerting.

Early in her years with Lord and Lady Henderson, Sadie realized that Lady Henderson and her lord differed from the couples she had met through the years or had an occasion to watch. Maybe it was the circle of friends the pair had, who seemed to enjoy quite distinct roles. The Lords were very interested in what their Ladies did and how they behaved. Or perhaps these pairs were the norm, and Sadie wasn't savvy enough or exposed enough to know, but she didn't see any two as loving as Lord and Lady Henderson besides, maybe, their friends.

One day, when Sadie was doing something for her mother, at around the age of eight, she went in search of the bedding in her ladyship's bedchamber when she heard her crying.

"I don't want to go to the party with those women, Papa. They are so rude." She heard several smacking sounds as though his lordship were laying his hand on his wife's posterior as most young children had experienced. Was he spanking his wife?

"That may well be, and I will take extra precautions to watch out for you, but we cannot stay home. Now dry your eyes and let papa make you feel better. Then you will put on your green dress. Wearing it always gives you more confidence, and you look beautiful in it. We leave in two hours, and if you dawdle in dressing, when we come home, papa will have no choice but to deal with your defiance."

"I'll be good for you. I don't like chastisements."

"No, I daresay not, but sometimes they make you feel so good, don't they?"

"Yes, papa," was her whispered reply.

When it grew quiet, Sadie tried hard to listen in, and other than rustling, a few moans, and heavy breathing, she heard nothing. Finally, there was movement, and after an adjoining door opened and closed, Sadie knocked timidly on Lady Clarise's door.

When she was bid to enter, the woman she saw in front of her was the same as she always had been. She wasn't that person whom Sadie had heard through the slightly open door. She was the woman Sadie had always known. Confused about what had gone on, Sadie never told another soul of the incident.

Over the years, as Sadie grew, she had been privy to many more occasions of cuddling and chastisements. She wanted that for herself one day, the cuddling, not the chastisements. His lordship adored his wife, and she, him. It seemed so unusual and yet entirely desirable. So many visitors to the house were cold and Sadie determined she would not marry a man or be such a woman as these.

One fateful evening, when the typical gentlemen visited his lordship, Sadie, now seventeen, listened to their conversation through a small opening in the drawing room servants' entrance. It was where the footmen or maids would go in and out without disturbing the inhabitants. She listened as the men spoke of their clubs, businesses, estates, lives, and lady loves. When the conversation moved to love, she wanted to ease away, but the words one man spoke struck a chord in her. He was a new participant in their discussions that evening, and his voice resonated throughout the room and with her.

"I'm not ready to find a wife, but when I am, how am I to find one who agrees with my particular choices? Few women would allow you to thrash them for disobedience even when you ensure they have pleasure with the pain."

"It can be hard," replied another. "The club is a good place to start. When you are ready, we shall gather at the tables and peruse the available women we know to be unattached, appropriate, and willing."

"It isn't how I found my wife," said one man. "She garnered my attention with her sassiness, and then I observed. Taking the plunge and smacking her arse was something of a risk, but it paid off."

Yet another said, "Nor I, but there is merit in settling on the necessary attributes and then assembling a list of ancillary desires. Certain telltale signs are often shared to help in the identification. You must be watchful and patient, but eventually, a little Darling will show herself. It is worth it."

The first man, whose laugh was rich and spine-tingling, spoke again. "Very well. When the time is right, I shall send you a message. Or maybe I'll look closer to home if I can find her with little fanfare."

"I'd be careful of that. You want your attributes kept behind closed doors, and doors in the country tend to resist staying closed. Especially with a local woman behind it."

Sadie imagined the inquiring man to be decisive in business and confident in himself, but one could only know precisely what the stock of a man was with proof. She wondered if he would be trustworthy and faithful to this mythical woman not yet found. What would it be like to have a man like that take to wife? Challenging.

His voice belied any weakness, so she envisioned him as being capable. A man to take charge. The very man she did not want to add to her forever. She wanted a man whose opinion sometimes ruled the day, one who was not too malleable, just comfortable. A man who thought she had a brain and could contribute to their life more than quietly running a household.

Maybe he would ask for her business opinion or estate business thoughts, but he would surely not expect her to do more than she was prepared to do. Best to find a husband who left her to her own devices most days. From what she heard, there was no man in attendance this evening with those attributes.

Soon, she saw the men sit down to dinner with Lord Henderson, but Lady Clarise did not attend. Sadie and her ladyship crossed paths with them after the two women had their dinner beside the fireplace. It was cold that night and the fire was cozy and warm. Sadie was careful not to discuss that she had been snooping. It was unladylike, and she did not want to do anything to upset Lady or Lord Henderson, so she said nothing. But the conversation was never far from her mind.

The men rose to leave just as Sarah's energy was flagging because of the late hour. She surreptitiously watched from the sitting room door as they prepared to leave, each accepting help with their greatcoat, having a last conversation before taking their leave of their host. Lady Henderson walked over behind Sadie, placing a gentle hand on her shoulder. Sadie jumped.

"It's unladylike to listen to men's conversations, my dear."

"I'm sorry, milady. I didn't mean to, but I own I am fascinated with them."

"It is rather interesting to see who has spent the evening with his lordship. Especially when they are young men, don't you think?" She shared a conspirator's smile with Sadie. "Now, which one do you think you would accept an offer from?"

"Oh, milady, I don't think I should even pretend that."

"Nonsense, it would be fun. Now that one in the back, the one that stands head and shoulders above the others. How about him?"

"No, because he is too tall and has a superior look about him. He wouldn't like a wife with an opinion."

"Hm, maybe, or maybe he has an exacting taste. Now, what about the well-dressed one with a broad smile?"

"Too frivolous. Likely to spend the family fortunes quickly."

"Yes, you might be right unless he has more than he can spend."

"Are there those who have that much?"

"Oh yes. See that gentleman with the interested look? He is as rich as Midas, I hear."

Sadie watched the man with strong carriage. His hair was the color of Swiss milk chocolate that she had been given as a treat last Christmas from Lady Clarise. His eyes were a blend of gold and green, his tall height, and his broad shoulders made to seem even broader with the physical pursuits he must engage in.

"I do find myself drawn to him. He seems to give everyone's words consideration. He might be willing to listen to a wife."

"Good choice. I believe Lord Henderson has said he is to be a duke one day. He is doing the work now, running the estate and making investments. I understand he is considered surprising because of some of his acquisitions, but he appears to land on his feet. His father has made some unfortunate choices, but his son has righted them. Lord Henderson has said on several occasions that the man is rather daring in his business ventures but is spot on most times earning him the nickname of the Daring Duke, even though he is not one yet. His name is Lord Griffin, I believe. He will be the Duke of Amesbury someday."

"Well then, out of my class, milady. As they all are."

"Perhaps, but not out of the realm of possibility, Sarah. Never forget that."

"Surely that would be a fallacy I should not entertain."

Lady Clarise hummed in a noncommittal response, confusing Sadie, so she put it all away as pipe dreaming. She would never have the opportunity to meet such a man, but she could look. Lord Henderson saw his wife and young Sarah behind her. He waved them over. Sadie hesitated.

"Come say goodnight, dear. And bring along Sarah." She had no choice but to comply.

Lord Henderson introduced every man as they took their leave. The only one who asked to take her hand was the man that had drawn her attention, introduced as Lord Griffin. Sadie tried to murmur platitudes as she did to the others, but he would have none of it. He leaned over her hand and kissed it. As the others talked while accepting and donning their coats and speaking to their hosts, and leaving, Lord Griffin continued to hold her hand and whispered, his voice carrying a gruff quality to it.

"Spying is naughty, Sarah. I heard you in the servant's entry and saw you in the corner before Lady Henderson found you. Should I punish you for those little indiscretions?" Sadie felt her middle cramp in what? Anticipation? Something flashed in his eyes. "Ah, I intrigued you."

All she could do was watch him, her eyes had always been expressive, and they connected to his. She held her quiet intake of breath in surprise. And attraction. And a tinge of fear.

"I didn't mean to offend you, milord," she murmured. "I was curious, but you are right. It was inappropriate for me to listen in on your conversation. Please forgive me."

"You do not offend. I daresay you could not. You enchant me, little one. It would seem that you might like my proposed chastisement. Would you like the feel of my hand on your backside, draped over my lap, my dear? Your gown lifted to show me where my hand shall land?"

Sadie felt her heart beat fiercely and so out of control that she feared it would burst.

"Please, sir."

He smiled. "You are delightful, my dear Sarah."

She could say nothing else, and he saved her from eternal mortification by acting as though he said nothing inappropriate or suggestive. He gave her a knowing smile and straightened.

"The pleasure is all mine, Sarah. Maybe we shall meet again, little one." Sadie didn't prefer to be called Sarah, but when Lord Griffin used her given name, she didn't mind.

She kept her eyes on him, even when Lord Henderson answered him cryptically, "It is possible."

Sadie determined that when she looked for a husband, Lord Griffin was the kind she wanted, even though a duke was so far above her station in life, it was laughable. Sadie knew there had to be more than one man like him in the world. There must be more than one man who looked into her eyes as though she had a brain and was worth knowing. Then the thought ignited such a burn in her deepest places that she could think of nothing else.

Finally, the gentlemen had all left for their own homes, and Lord Henderson sent Sadie to her room after seeing to Lady Clarise's bedtime routines. Finally, alone, Sadie thought of how her very center was in turmoil in the presence of Lord Griffin. Even though he was not yet a duke, it was in his future, and therefore he was not in hers. Sadie tried to think of what she liked about him and thought it more productive to think about what didn't attract her.

Well, very little could be said against the young lord except that he called her 'little one' as though she were a child. She was nearly eighteen. That was a young lady in any circle. And he asked if he should punish her. The mere thought made her cheeks flame. She did love his voice, relishing the excitement that sent delightful shivers up her back and down her center, settling in very intimate places. And what did Lord Henderson mean by his "it is possible" reply when Lord Griffin suggested another meeting?

Sadie rolled over and dreamed of her knight in shining armor with a deep voice, rich brown hair, and unique eye color. Her knight was tall, but what was more profound was his bulk and his overall presence in the room. Even in her dreams, her belly quivered, and her intimate area was wet and tingling at the vision of him.

Chapter 1 Time For Discovery

The next morning, as Lady Clarise made herself, and by default Sadie, available for visitors, Lord Griffin, his sister, and his mother came to call on Lord and Lady Henderson. It was unusual because when the duchess came, it had been her son's habit to never attend visits, but on this occasion, he broke with that tradition, much to everyone's surprise. His sister Julia seemed bored, as was usual. There were no young men to take her attention, so she saw no value in the visit.

This morning, the duchess was reacquainting herself with her friends, none, it seemed, who had eligible sons to take her daughter's interest. Lady Julia's temper was on display, but she took a turn around the room with Sadie and then moved to the side as her brother moved alongside Sadie to speak. He stopped to whisper something in his sibling's ear and she shook her head in response. His raised brow and her sign of discontent ended the one-sided conversation. Julia returned to her mother's side.

Lord Griffin offered his arm and Sadie looked over at Lady Clarise who raised one slender brow. That was all Sadie needed to clasp her hands in front of her instead of taking his arm.

"I don't believe Lady Clarise believes I should take your arm. Newly introduced people, especially male to female, should not touch in that way."

"Of course, they do. If I were to escort you into dinner, say, I would offer my arm and you would be obliged to take it."

"Perchance we would attempt that on your next visit, milord."

"Perhaps. Shall we take a few turns about the room?"

"Four."

"Four turns? Is that a rule?"

"No, well, I suppose it is. It takes four turns of the room to be considered a good visit."

Sadie spoke with clear authority on the subject. Lord Griffin tried to mask his smile but was woefully unsuccessful. They took four turns about the room exactly. The time for a respectable visit between the two of them without drawing suspicion. Or so Sadie thought.

"My dear Sarah, I believe I understood Lord Henderson to say you are not yet eighteen."

Sadie's expression hardened as she turned to look at her companion. "Do you always discuss a lady's age, sir?"

Richard tsked. "Such a sharp tongue for such a delicate lady. I shall enjoy taming its tartness. And, to answer your question, no, I have rarely discussed a woman's age, but I have never been interested in a young lady as much as you take my attention."

Sadie sighed. "I fear you waste your time, milord, for I am no lady of title. And certainly, unable to be a duchess. We can be little more than friends."

"So, you have heard I am to be a duke someday. That means I choose my wife; my wife does not choose me."

Sadie laughed as discreetly as she was able. "I hear you are a duke in all but title now. A wealthy one at that. Commendable, I am told. His lordship holds you in great regard; however, that mandates you marry well, meaning you are required to choose from a specific pool of women."

"Does he... say complimentary things? I am honored to be looked upon so generously. And how do you hold me, Sarah? Am I also in your high regard?" Richard sent a glance in Sadie's direction before turning to look ahead.

"Sir, I said more than that. You must attend if we are to do well together. I cannot say at present my level esteem. How should I hold you, milord?"

"With interest, and maybe desire? Does Lord Henderson say you are unsuited to be a duchess?" Sadie noticed his voice hardened, and she felt she should defend her lordship.

"No, he has said nothing of the kind, for we do not discuss such things. However, it is obvious that must be the case. A duke must marry similar in rank. I am not unschooled in society's peculiarities."

"Oh? What peculiarities?"

She could hear the interest in his tone. Sadie could feel the heat in her cheeks; indeed, her whole body was heated. She experienced small tremors at the indiscretion of her words.

"I cannot, milord." He smiled. Was it her hushed whisper or her blush. He was a most unkind man to not ignore the whole so she could relax and save face.

"No? Well, we shall tease those out at another time, Sarah. Society is not the only one with certain peculiarities."

Sadie thought of what she had overheard in Lady Henderson's chambers that evening long ago. "Yes, I believe that to be true."

He searched her face. "Yes, Sarah, I believe you do."

"Sadie. Lord and Lady Henderson believe Sarah is a dignified name, but I think it is used too often. Do you not agree? Sadie is a unique rendition of Sarah. When we are alone, I prefer Sadie."

"Unique like you." He seemed to ponder the idea of Sarah being Sadie. "Yes, I believe you could be a Sadie rather than Sarah sometimes." He almost smiled. "In fact, I rather believe you are more often Sadie."

Sadie hesitated, not sure what he exactly meant, but at least he agreed. "In my heart, I most definitely am. In my public self, I am told I cannot be. Therefore, I am not."

"So, you do conform to social edicts."

"Not conform, bow."

Sadie continued to look forward as she spoke to Richard, with few times to study him, as was proper. The urge, however, to stare at him with focused attention was intense. Convention was very intrusive and difficult to understand when you were being dictated by it.

"Is that not splitting hairs? Do you always bow to the conventions of the day?" It was as though he knew her thoughts.

"Am I not supposed to do so?"

"Sometimes, little one. Sometimes."

"In truth, I may bow to convention on the occasion for I am not a fool, but it is a momentary bow, I assure you."

They continued to saunter around the room. "Then, in private, intimate conversations, may I invite you to call me Richard? It is who I am when not in the public forum."

"Yes, except, isn't that being very improper? Your title being marquess until you are a duke?"

"No more improper than calling you Sadie before we have an understanding."

"Oh. Well, there is no harm, I suppose. Do you reside in London, sir?"

"Nice diversion transition from private to proper. You will do well as a woman in society. But to answer your question, I am in London for a season, typically. I have been known to travel here one time before year end as well but not always. I may want to do that now that I have met you, if you would be open to that."

"I would like that, milord."

"Our family estate is in Wiltshire. A beautiful part of the country. Have you been?"

"I've not left London, but I'm sure it is lovely."

"Maybe I will take you someday. Yes, I believe I will if you are in agreement."

She turned to see if Richard was teasing. He didn't seem to be, and she stopped walking. "I would love to see it." She deflated a little. "But it would be improper."

"Keep walking, my dear, or you will draw attention to us. And it would not be improper if you were to become my wife or my betrothed."

Sadie stopped again. "But I cannot. You are a lord that will be a duke. I am... nothing."

"If you don't want a thrashing for such sentiments, you will not say them again. I will not tolerate anyone speaking ill of you, not even yourself."

Immediately chastised, Sadie replied, subdued. "Yes, milord."

"Very prettily done, my sweet. Now, keep walking, my dear."

Sadie began walking again. "Stop teasing me, milord. It is distasteful." Her manner was said she aggravated that his lordship must have thought that dangling being with him when it was impossible, funny.

"I promise I do not. It is too early to see if we would suit, but I shall pursue the possibility in earnest when you are of proper age, and we become better acquainted. We will see if we do well together. When I believe you are ready, and not before. Until that time comes, I will continue to spend time with you, and once I leave London for the country, I will stay in contact."

"You would write to me, sir?" Her surprise was evident in her voice.

Richard chuckled. "Do you doubt my ability to do so? I am schooled, my dear. Then when I return, we will continue our friendship. I shall ask for your hand if we suit and take you with me, if you are ready."

"Why can you not take me now? I might disagree that we suit later."

"Ah, and that is where my title and position will win out, my dear. Never doubt, my dear will be mine if I should want you as my Darling Duchess. But I would never force you. I would never take you before you are ready but have no doubt, you will be mine, princess."

"I should say not. And what if I am not agreeable? How would you reconcile yourself to not getting whatever you desire?"

"I don't anticipate that being a problem, princess. My powers of persuasion would do the work, princess." His smile was as maddening as it was enticing.

"You are quite prideful. I should be careful of my words, sir. And princess is not an endearment, sir. It is meant in a taunting way. I prefer Sadie."

"Not at all, my dear. I enjoy using endearments and all are meant in affection, I assure you, Sadie."

The fourth turn about the room was over, and the Griffins took their leave. "Until our paths cross again, my dear." Richard kissed her hand again, lingering for a long moment. Just as it was becoming improper, he released her.

Richard came back many more times during that spring and summer, and each time he was more and more familiar, asking Sadie personal questions such as, "Would you enjoy being a lady if you had the opportunity?"

And each time, she answered the queries as honestly as she could. She wondered why her ladyship allowed the familiarity, but Lord Henderson would come to the garden, where she and Richard often met, and take a walk with his wife, giving them quiet but supervised time.

"I don't know if I want to be a lady. There are too many rules to live by. I believe it would be too hard for me."

Richard seemed to hesitate for a moment. "I was under the impression that Lady Henderson instructed you on such matters."

"Oh, she has, but I am not naïve, sir. I know it takes much of her time to ensure she is following the rules and expectations set out by society. It isn't simply overseeing one's home. That is easy. I am not sure I care to burden myself with such mandates as whom to friendly with, and whom you should invite to gatherings, and what type of invitation to reciprocate."

"There is no denying that it takes considerable time, but surely if you know what to do, the overall task is not that difficult. As you say, running your house is straightforward, but the nuance of etiquette is trickier. I would be there to help you."

Sadie smiled and shook her head. "I fear you have been misinformed, milord. Am I to understand that you believe the house to run itself with little effort? For I assure you, that would be a misconception. I am meant to say that it is not necessary to be a slave to others' expectations. If you know what is important to you and do that thing rather than all others, life should be as you wish it to be, however that luxury is not reality. You would not always be available to lighten the burden, nor would you want to be. I am saying, I'm not sure I would want such a heaviness."

He gave her a mock bow. "You believe me to be mistaken, and you are offended. You do not lean on good manners if you would argue with me at every turn. I do have a solution to that fault."

"I bid you a good day, sir."

Sadie turned to leave, but Richard grabbed her hand and drew her closer to him. He caressed her cheek and kissed it.

"You are a spicy one and that excites me, but I will not allow you to get away with such mouthiness without consequences." He leaned in so his hot breath bathed her cheek. His hand slid to her backside, he patted her quivering flesh through the dress and grinned.

"Shall I spank your attitude away, little one? Arguing with me at every turn is not done, Sadie. If you were mine, this dress would be pushed away and your little sit-upon would be quickly peppered with attention from my hand. My duchess would behave or face the consequences."

She felt the heat rise to her cheeks, heard her name on his lips, and the strength of his personality, causing her intimate places to twist and twirl. "I... milord, please do not say such things." Her whisper held an element of desperation in it. To be heard would ruin her reputation and enhance his.

Richard gentled his tone and his hold on her. "Why not, Sadie? Does it excite you? Are you tingling in places you haven't explored yet? Are there butterflies in your middle? That is desire, my dear. I could share with you how to build and answer those desires when you are older."

"Yesss." She took in a deep breath and slowly released it. Time she changed the subject. "Is there an accepted year that one could experience those things? I am seventeen, milord. Quite of an age to know all manner of things."

"When you are ready."

Sadie crossed her arms and stopped their walk to give him a pouty face of disagreement.

"Sadie, I will know when you are ready for a papa. Do not defy me in this. Resume walking, princess, or I shall have to leave."

"Then leave. I do not care about your decisions. I am not yours to command, milord."

His voice softened. "Not now, my darling girl. Now you feel I have rejected you, but I have not. I am not doing this to cause you grief. Rest assured that there will come a day when that will not be a genuine sentiment because you will be happy to receive me and there will be nothing to stand in your way or mine."

He gave Sadie a slight bow, took his leave of Lord and Lady Henderson, and left. Sadie took her leave as well, rushing from the library and racing to her room to cry out her despair at her turning Richard away.

Lord Henderson never spoke of Richard's visits, but he did allow them. Richard visited several more times before he left the city for the country. During the following year, when the Spring brought Lord Griffin, the same exchanges ensued. Only the visits fell into a weekly pattern Sadie looked forward to. Lord Griffin became bolder and bolder each visit until one day when Sadie was in a particularly sour mood, he declared she had earned her first punishment at his hand. He immediately sat her on the bench beneath some heavy greenery and left to seek her benefactors.

Sadie's worry grew until she was sick with it. She thought to leave every moment but did not want to upset him more, so she waited. As she watched for him, she finally spied him returning with purpose, and she was sure Lord Henderson would accompany him, ready to mete out her penalty for being so rude to a guest, but that did not happen.

"Lord Henderson has given his permission for your punishment," Richard announced as he sat on the stone bench next to Sadie, who stood immediately.

"I do not believe you, nor do I agree. What do you mean to do?"

"Warm your sit-upon, princess. You are behaving like my little duchess and so you will be treated as such."

"No, I don't agree. You shan't lay a hand on me, sir."

"Yes, when you are in the suds, Sadie, it is preferred that you refer to me as my lord or sir."

He reached for her wrist and pulled her over his knee with such smooth efficiency that Sadie thought he must be inappropriate with a great number of young ladies. She kicked and was quite surprised at the strength of the man.

"We are not kin, sir. This is highly inappropriate!"

"And embarrassing, I imagine, which is expected. Preferable, in fact. Sadie, if you wish for the world to hear of your punishment, then you are free to kick up a commotion. However, if you wish this chastisement to be between us, you will take your punishment like a lady and keep quiet. Although, after the nastiness that you have displayed today, I rather expect you to release a storehouse of screams designed to bring in your benefactor. I assure you that Lord Henderson will not come to your rescue, for he agreed to this course of action. Now I need you to agree."

"Well, I do not."

"Sadie, as much as I understand the circumstances you find yourself in, it is of your own doing. I had thought you more honorable than evading just punishment for your purposeful deeds. Am I mistaken in my reading of your character?"

She sighed. "You are not, sir. I agree to punishment, but not of this kind. Is there no other way?" she pleaded.

"I will make this better than you can imagine."

"I can't envision this situation to be better."

"Do you trust me, princess?"

"Yes," she answered swiftly. "But remember decorum, sir."

"I will do my best, my dear."

Richard smoothed her light summer dress over her enticing derriere, warming the striking zone with slow circles of her striking zone. At first Sadie was tense but his hand lulled her into a since of complacency and she relaxed. The bench was low enough and she was just tall enough to touch her toes to the ground. He tipped her so her fingers touched, and her feet did not make purchase with the ground.

His demeanor changed and Sadie kicked her legs and heard just before she felt the sting of his hand on her thigh. "Sir, please. I apologize."

"The time for apologies is over, my dear. Remember, there are many listening ears. I can imagine that if they hear your suffering, they will come and investigate your distress. The shame, I daresay, will be intense. Likely, much worse than the punishment itself."

Another smack landed, this time on the full of her arse. She swallowed the scream she wanted to release. She bit down on his thigh instead and was rewarded with a flurry of swats that landed hard on her rear quadrant. Then he rubbed again.

"Lady Sarah, that bite was unladylike and inadvisable. Should you repeat it, I shall strip your gown from your body and take my strap to you, and then claim you as mine today, regardless of your age or life experiences. Am I clear?"

All the while he spoke, his hand bounced off her delicate backside and her cries were as muffled as she could keep them. She was mortified, angry, sorrowful, regretful, and a whole slew of other emotions she wasn't sure she could identify properly. And what horrified her is that she wanted him to claim her. Not take a strap to her but take her. What must she be thinking? This punishment was not having the desired effect if she was supposed to hate the feel of his hand on her backside.

This man was insufferable, and yet, when his hand came dangerously close to the tender flesh between her legs, even though she was completely covered, the thought was mortifying and enticing. She would do all he asked if he would but ask. Tears flowed unchecked fueled by the increasing heat where his hand was landing and her confusion. When she kicked her legs in frustration, he spanked her thighs. The heat grew, and the pain increased until she sobbed her sincere regret for disrespecting him.

Immediately, her punisher became her soother. He lifted Sadie into his arms and onto his lap, careful not to place too much pressure on her newly punished backside. He kissed her cheeks, her hair, her lips. The kisses were mere pressing of his lips to her and then done but it was intense in the reaction her body had.

"Sir, I can't... it's so much."

"There, there, my love. Papa is proud of you for taking your punishment so well. What a brave girl." He kissed her lips again for a less hurried moment. "My sweetheart, I'm not sure I can allow you to be away from me for another winter. I want you, my princess. You need your Papa to claim you."

"I want you, too, milord." She hiccupped and sniffled. "You said I wasn't old enough for a papa."

He continued to rub her back and kiss her hair, rocking and comforting her. "Clever girl, to remember that. I believe you are old enough now."

Sadie's tears soon subsided. "Because I am eighteen now?"

"Because you are mine."

An incredible feeling of protection and rightness permeated her being. She listened to his words. Her Papa, his little one, mine, were all words he used and they made her feel so protected. Wanted. She belonged to him as sure as if she were married today. The excitement that came from his hand landing on her What did that mean? And was it the same thing that Richard had referred to as his peculiarities? Was this what married life was about?

Her posterior wasn't the only thing throbbing, her center was vibrating. "Milord, it feels, odd."

"That is your desire thrumming through your body. You enjoyed that spanking and then the caresses afterwards. We are made for the other, princess. I mean for us to marry. Do not accept any advances for any other for I would have to challenge them, and I don't wish to do that. Wait for me."

"I shall endeavor to not excite your ire, sir." Sadie fixed him with her grin.

"Yes, see that you don't, my little imp." He laughed, his voice rich and resonate. Richard sobered and said, "My sweet, listen to my words. I need to go back to my home but when I return, I am claiming you and taking you to Amesbury House with me. Be prepared, my love. If, while I am gone, that you ever need anything, send me word and if it is immediate, I will leave you the addresses of my friends who live in London. Make use of them to meet your needs. They are well aware of my feelings for you."

She agreed but Sadie wasn't someone to ask for help. She muddled through or figured it out herself. Knowing Richard, however, that would never do so she simply agreed.

Richard soon went back to his estate in the country, but the words he used, the feelings they invoked, and the emptiness she felt this time when he had gone, left her confused, hungry... and curious. What would it be like to truly be Lady Griffin? Or, as he referred to her, his Darling Duchess? Would it be giving up too much for that privilege, if indeed it was a privilege?

Only time would tell. His next visit would be the deciding factor.

Chapter 2 Time to Mourn

The following autumn, several months after Lord Griffin left London for his country home for a second year after spending time with Sadie, Lady Clarise fell very ill. No matter the amount of care she received, or the prayers the house sent up, she was gone before Sadie's nineteenth birthday. Lord Henderson had requested no visitors for his year of mourning, and that included Lord Griffin.

When Sadie brought up meeting the viscount in the park or other place, with escort, Lord Henderson denied it out of hand. She was distraught with the man she couldn't get out of her mind, so close and yet out of reach, but Richard sent her letters of encouragement. He finished his time in London early, and since his mother and sister left early, and he could not visit with Sadie, he left as well.

Sadie received continued notes of his regards and sympathies, an occasional letter along with sweets and fruit when available, but he did not return when the year of mourning was done, to speak with her that year. Sadie felt sure that was the end of any hope of continuing their acquaintance.

The following year, when Richard would have come in the late winter of the year, he received word that his father had passed away. While Richard had been working the estate as though his father had already died, it was proper to grieve him. Sadie did not begrudge him in his mourning or his additional work to completely take over his father's affairs, but she did feel thwarted, and her mood became very low.

Richard refused to allow his father's stipend to continue to his mistress. That woman was angry, but Richard was equally angry on his mother's behalf to care very much. Some ugly rumors were surfacing in London on that score, as the mistress did not go away quietly. Richard had sent an urgent message to

Lord Henderson and begged that he keep Sarah from the distastefulness of the situation until he could explain in person.

His lordship wasn't entirely successful, but he did his best. While Richard kept in touch during the following spring and summer, there was to be no face-to-face time. He didn't come that year as another autumn passed, and Sadie turned twenty. Richard's letters were regularly received, and he comforted her and reassured her, but it had been two years since she had seen him. The genuine fear that he had grown past his need for her was a strong dread in her soul.

Another year of mourning ensued, and Sadie grew restless. She sent letters to Richard. He continued with the sweets and other treats, but he did not mention the familiarity that had passed between them. She feared he regretted it. It had been too long since they had laid eyes on each other. After all, she was a full twenty years of age now and possibly he had found another.

In the new year, with the snow on the ground and the winds so cold it froze a person to their very soul, Lord Henderson left this earth to be with his beloved. While Sadie was happy for him to be reunited with his love, it was a scary time for Sadie. Lord Henderson passed so quickly that there was little opportunity to prepare herself.

At the moment of his death, she had too much to do to succumb to her immense grief or process what this meant for her. That would come when she had completed the tasks laid before her. Sadie had specific instructions from Lord Henderson and would not fail him.

So, even before others knew he was dead, and long before his body turned cold, Sadie began fulfilling the elder's requests of her. Lord Henderson had given Sadie strict instructions on what to remove from his desk the moment she knew he was gone from this earth.

"Do not spare a tear, my dear, until you have done all I have instructed, for I promise you there will be mayhem if you veer from these things."

Sadie waited until he took his last breath, then she informed the footman outside the room that his lordship was taking a nap. Then she slipped downstairs, through the servant's back hall entrance, and began her work. She then gathered all the things he had drilled into her, the good account books, not the skeleton set he had for when others would look through them after his death. He didn't want anyone to know his true wealth pertaining to the townhouse, in particular. Sadie didn't know why and would never have dared ask. Now it didn't matter.

She gathered the money he had in his library desk, not his study, leaving precisely the amount he instructed for staff wages, and put the rest into the place he had shown her for safekeeping. Safekeeping for whom she did not know, but she did everything he requested precisely as he had asked.

Then, when she had finished his instructions, she reappeared in his bedroom, announced his death, and waited for the doctor to arrive. That good man verified that there was no life and nothing he could do. Sadie waited until the undertaker arrived for his body measurements before she went into her room, locked the door, and cried. She didn't leave for the rest of the day.

Tomorrow would be soon enough to greet the mourners wishing to visit. It was winter, and Mrs. Arnold reminded Sadie that there wouldn't be as many callers as might have attended in the better weather months. But London was dreary all times of the year and if a person was intent on paying their respects, they would.

"And there will likely be no family in attendance. Lord Henderson's brother has never once put in an appearance as long as I have been here and your mother never mentioned it either. I imagine the solicitor will handle all." That matronly woman shook her head in disbelief.

Now, a full day later, when the house was in such a bustle over the loss of their employer, Sadie organized things as they taught her. And just as Lord Henderson had instructed, Sadie sent word to Mr. Shackleford, the solicitor, who organized the next events.

Sadie looked over the house full of scurrying staff that once served Lord and Lady Henderson, now preparing the townhouse for later sale. The atmosphere was one of sadness, for Lord and Lady Henderson were good employers. Apprehension, excitement, and fear mingled in with an air of determination to do their best last act of service for Lord and Lady Henderson.

The day was dreary, cold, and damp when Lord Henderson was laid to rest next to his love. Only the staff, a couple of mourners, a few parishioners that Sadie wondered if they were paid to attend funerals, and the solicitor, Mr. Shackelford. It was a hard day. Sadie's life was such a mess.

After the short graveside service, she sat in the library and inhaled her benefactor's scent. He was the only experience of a father she had, save for the butler

Mr. Arnold, who did the best he could, given his position. It was Mr. Arnold who had encouraged her to accept the generosity of his lordship.

Would Richard come now? She would send him a letter once they settled things, and she had done all that Lord Henderson instructed her to do. As she sat in the library and contemplated the promises he had spoken to her, the last time they had seen each other, she experienced her own bit of fear and uncertainty. He had entreated her to use his services, no matter the circumstances, if she needed him. He also gave her several residents' names in London for immediate help, but Sadie had known then as now that she would not avail herself of those connections.

She was not left without resources, but it had been two and a half years since she had seen her lord now a duke's face and heard the sound of his voice. So much had passed in their lives. Would he remember her look, her voice? Would they still please him? She could remember every detail of the last visit. He used his words of endearment to reassure her and touches that now echoed in her mind.

The implication of his words seared in her memory, and the feeling of warmth seeped into her chilled body and spirit. She had heard those same words of comfort and protection when Lord Henderson was speaking with Lady Henderson. It meant something to them. She wanted them to mean something to her.

Sadie tried to recall the conversation she had overheard between Mr. and Mrs. Arnold. It had been some years ago, but now the incident became a clear memory.

"Don't you think she is getting too old for his lordship to chastise? Physically, I mean?"

"Not if they enjoy the way it makes them connect in their alone time, Mrs. A. And he only uses his hand. I think it is none of our business."

"But surely, Mr. Arnold, it is odd to treat her like a princess when she is in her sixtieth year and then chastise her when she chooses not to follow his wishes."

"Do you think she is unhappy?"

"That's the strange bit. She isn't. She is like a woman in her youth when he is around her. When there is no company or guests, they are playing as though she is but a girl, and he is her stern papa."

"Or loving papa. I believe it is the reason they still visit each other in the night. Maybe it would be a good idea to learn from them, and maybe you would be hesitant to deny me so often, madam."

"I should scream the house down if you were to take your strap to me, sir."

"Aye, maybe. But maybe you would be better behaved and more compliant."

She heard them both laugh, and it was quiet for a moment before she heard, "That is all you are getting from me in the middle of a day, sir. Now, off with you."

"Maybe tonight I will lay my leather on your backside and heat things up."

"Or maybe just your hand, sir."

Mr. Arnold laughed again before heading toward the door, and Sadie nearly didn't slip into the paneled compartment in time. Getting caught during that conversation would have been unforgivable and she would never have lived down the utter mortification. Couples were an odd lot. Richard would come when he found out she needed him. She prayed she was right. Staying alone was too frightening to contemplate for long.

When Lady Henderson became mortally ill, she went downhill fast. His lordship was so kind to her and stayed by her side, but he allowed Sadie to sit with them. More often than not, she had meals with them in her lady's sitting room, and his lordship held his wife as she cuddled in his lap. On that last day, he sent Sadie out of the room and told her to wait until he sent for her. She kissed Lady Clarise and walked out. Tears streamed as she made her last goodbye. She wanted that kind of love and commitment to a lover.

In the late afternoon, Lord Henderson told Sadie that his wife had gone to sleep. Then he went to his bed, in his own room, for the first time since his wife had grown ill weeks before. After that day, the old lord had not let Sadie out of his sight and even, toward the end, called her Clarise, his wife's name.

Recently, when Lord Henderson's health and mind declined, he chastised her when she hesitated to do something and threatened to take her in hand. He even referred to himself as her papa once in those last hours. It should have been difficult to deal with that behavior in her benefactor, but she remembered how compatible the two were and how much they loved each other. She would put up with all manner of nonsense if her husband loved her as his lordship loved his wife. Is that what Richard had meant?

One day, his lordship spoke to her as the young woman she had become. His message was clear and sound.

"Sarah, my dear, I have something I want to tell you." Using her Christian name meant he was serious. "Men can be bores, and they can be cruel if they are not well brought up. They are often beyond the pale if they do not check their behaviors. I don't wish that embarrassment or pain for you. You have no father or mother to share the things you should know about in the need to find a good husband. It is of the utmost importance that you choose carefully and accept that a man who loves his wife will take the time to chastise her if she requires it."

"Yes, milord."

What else could she say? Not that she did not hold Lord Henderson in great regard, but he was wrong. Richard seemed to believe the same thing as his punishment proved, but it left her with comfort, protection. Could this be what was going on in their mind? Could that be the meaning behind the chastisements, raised brows, changed behaviors and submissive behavior?

She did not have to submit to discipline from her husband. It was an accepted practice, after all. The less refined, the more likely, but she had determined not to allow it in her marriage, except what if letting him take control was the secret to a loving marriage. Not the punishments but the security of it all.

"You think I am wrong, but if a man doesn't protect you, guide you, or expect your best, then he is not the man for you. Better he takes his hand to your sit-upon when you put yourself in harm's way than not care a whit about you."

"Yes, milord."

Sadie had been the recipient of such behavior correction, and she had not enjoyed it. Thoughts of Richard, the lord who would be a duke, came to mind. The scolding would have been hard enough to bear, but his spanking was a sweet torture. Regardless, or maybe because of the unfathomable feelings inside that she experienced when taking her chastisement, she would not have it. She needed to keep control.

"Promise me you will not align yourself with any man that is not thoroughly watchful and enamored of you. Who takes a very strong interest in everything concerning you. Who makes you feel well-loved."

Since she did not believe she would ever find a man to her liking if Richard did not follow through, promising was easy. "I promise, milord."

The old man grunted his approval. "And another thing, if you should find such a man, he is likely to be one that will pull you over his lap for an earned thrashing and into his lap for a cuddle. Don't deny him. And if he seems to be a bit odd in some of his requests, hear him out. You won't be sorry you did."

Not knowing what to make of the old gentleman's admonishment, she nodded. "Yes, milord."

He patted her knee paternally and gazed off for a moment. "I might be able to help you in that regard," he said, more to himself than to her. "If one comes to offer himself to you and I am not here to receive him, remember my words."

He then instructed her on what to do when he passed from this earth with clarity and determination. Once he was through and seemingly resolved about something, he dismissed her. "Now, off with you. I have work to do, and you are hindering my progress," he said gruffly to cover his uncharacteristic bout of emotion.

What work he intended to do in his bed, she had no clue, but he called his valet and shooed her from the room.

Sadie had grown to love the gentleman and his annoyance at the breakthroughs of such an unmanly display. Several months later, in an uncharacteristic burst of energy and clarity, he made Sadie go for a walk with him into the garden.

"I am getting old, my dear."

"Nonsense, milord."

"Oh, it is true, and well we both know it. I was a full ten years older than my dear Clarise and I've lost her. I'll soon be eighty and I am growing tired. Men don't need companions and certainly not young ladies, but we like them. Sit with me for a while, my dear."

They sat on one of the many benches in the garden enjoying the lack of rain that day.

"What is wrong, milord? You seem sad, somehow."

"You are so watchful, my dear Sarah. I prefer you to any other person in my home. Most of my dear friends are gone or, like me, are unable and unwilling to travel. I daresay you have things you would rather do but indulge me for the time I have left, my dear. I will leave you well provided for in the box that

I buried in the garden soon after your mother passed from this earth, and you began lifting my Clarise's spirits with your attentions. Just over there, under the juniper tree, beneath the bench."

"Milord don't worry about me. I'll get along fine. I'm quite self-sufficient, and Lady Clarise has taught me many things. Besides, you must be around to peruse my male suitors."

"I do not doubt your ingenuity, my dear Sadie. As far as a suitor and marriage, I have done some groundwork in preparation for your happiness, but if I cannot meet that obligation, promise me you will grab the box. Wait until the servants are all gone, because if you don't, they will take the inheritance I have left for you. Clarise would not have approved of the amount put aside for you, but my dear wife wasn't privy to many things I did over the years. There is no one left who might know about the box, so no one to be concerned about in that regard. Promise me you will take it."

"I promise, sir. But why would Lady Clarise have a differing opinion? And maybe she was right?"

"She loved you almost like her own. But the reality is that my wife was raised strictly and to go against convention was not allowed." He shrugged. "I was raised to think my own way and I hope, with all my teaching in all manner of business these last years, you will not feel too hesitant to choose your own path. Quietly, of course. But I wish for you to spread your wings, but only a little. It won't do to fly too much in the face of conventions and society."

"Yes, milord."

"One last thing. I know you have had a tender heart for our Duke of Amesbury. If he should offer, consider it well. He is a good man, and a kind soul. He will make every dream you ever had come true. Most of all, you will always be secure in his affections and your care."

"If he would only declare, milord."

He patted Sadie's hand. "Do not despair. There's a dear. Now run along. I need to go inside and rest my eyes."

Lord Henderson never admitted to napping. She never thought that he had really buried a box of money or anything, and, before too long, forgot about it entirely.

But now the old gentleman was dead. Just before he passed, he whispered to her, "Remember. Under the bench below the juniper tree. Let no one know.

I have left you a few bobs in the will, but your real treasure is beneath the tree, my dear. Use it wisely, as I have taught you. And never fear, I have sent for your husband. You will know him when you see him."

The outrage she might have felt at the elderly lord endeavoring to find her a husband or acting on that discovery of the perfect man, according to him, was mitigated by the fact that he was so ill and now lay dead.

Sadie, like all the rest of the staff, received a modest bit of money to compensate for the immediate loss of income that occurred when Lord Henderson died. A couple of staff were asked to stay an extra fortnight to right the house, some had found employment immediately, and others promised to attend the funeral, but other than that, the rented townhouse was empty within a few days of his death.

Since the couple had no children, his lordship, having given the ancestral home to his brother and his large family, the bulk of Lord Henderson's estate was shifted to his brother and one sister living in the north near Scotland. The old man had also left a portion to Sadie's long-dead mother, whom he pretended not to know was dead. As per custom, that amount went to Sadie, and he specifically left instructions with his solicitor that Sadie was to stay in the home and be the last to leave.

The other employees were not privy to Sadie's last instructions, or the extra funds left to her through her mother. The solicitor, Mr. Shackleford, was very discreet in all matters, sharing only what each received in wages, a small extra bit, and a glowing letter of recommendation to the individual they were directed to. So, if anyone knew of another's bequeath, it was because that person shared it.

There were a few who grumbled when Sadie didn't leave with them, but the solicitor, who had proven his discretion, could also be quite commanding when the situation called for it. He directed the exit of the rest of the staff. There was still a small bit of grumbling, but no one carried their disgruntled behavior further, for which Sadie was grateful. She was feeling very vulnerable and nearly agreed to go with the others to one of their new households, but the last conversation with the elder prompted her to follow his instructions.

She had already formulated a story to appease the group.

"I have a new position that Lord Henderson gained for me to begin after his death. It involves children which I am happy about. I've never met them, but he sent them a letter of reference and received acceptance. Mr. Shackleford has sent off the information that I am now available and expect to be retrieved within the month."

It wasn't wrong if you looked at it with your head tilted. Husband chosen if she accepted him; he was coming for her, there would be the anticipation of children. All true, in a kind of way.

The older gentleman frowned at the balderdash she was dishing up, but he offered no words of contradiction. Maybe he too could see her thinking. Sadie felt guilty lying, but there was nothing for it. To accomplish what Lord Henderson had tasked her to do, she had no other alternative.

Mrs. Arnold looked so relieved. "Oh, my dear girl, that is perfect for you. You have such a kind heart and love children. I worried about you not finding a position for yourself. A governess will be the best way to find a husband who is good to you. Yes," Mrs. Arnold nodded, "it was the best choice."

"Yes, I agree."

As she thought more about it and no one appeared to at least be introduced to her, Sadie began to think she wasn't ready to marry anyone, especially someone of another's choosing. She had chosen Richard but of course, it was a pipe dream. She would communicate that Lord Henderson had been mistaken, if someone showed up to retrieve her.

Sadie's heart was pounding because it felt as though her deception would be found out before the household went to their new employment, but it never happened. The parting was tearful and difficult, and she promised to write when she was able.

"And you never know, I might stop in and see you and share a cup of tea someday, Mrs. A."

When all was ready, the last employees began leaving throughout the day until it was only Sadie and the Arnolds left. When Mrs. Arnold was ready to go, she left her with some advice.

"You are now to present as Sarah. Sadie was the child version of you which you must put away. Life isn't protective, as we have strived to be for you as you grew into this incredible, capable woman. Do not forget to be a lady, regardless of your station. It will serve you well. You will teach children their deportment and manners, so you must be very careful with yours. My girth is too grand, so you make sure to go and get her ladyship's gowns and make use of them. Take all the very nicest ones, for you never know when your prince will arrive."

"I will."

"And pack them all in a nice trunk or even two. Take the hair combs and whatever accessories you like. The solicitor or Lord Henderson's brother will sell them if you do not or give the lot to the poor, for we know there are no other relatives. You are taking care of some of the solicitor's work for him by doing that. And finally, find yourself a man you love and that loves you. Like his lordship and her ladyship. Or like Mr. Arnold and myself. Then do whatever is necessary to keep him satisfied."

"I will, I promise. I'm going to miss you and Mr. Arnold."

"It's like leaving my own child." The housekeeper sniffled. "Remember where we are and come visit if you can."

Mr. Arnold cleared his throat. "We need to go, my dear. Our employers will wonder if we are coming at all if we wait longer."

Lord Henderson had made sure the couple went to their new employers with an excellent reference. The Arnold's receiving employer would never find a better couple to run their house and Sadie knew it. She was happy for them going to another household that appreciated them as they were here. She wished they would stay with her but with no home to speak of yet, that was impossible.

Mrs. Arnold nodded. The women hugged. She clasped Sadie to her bosom as they sniffed. Then the couple was gone and the only one in the big, cavernous house was Sadie. She was never so bereft in her life as at that very moment. She allowed herself to succumb to the tears that flowed freely down her face.

The library sofa was where she napped later that afternoon. The same sofa she had sat on, beside his lordship so many times after his wife had passed as they drank tea, even chocolate, and Sadie listened as the elderly gentleman talked. She could hear his words of warning and instruction. She heard his voice as clearly as if he were still in the room with her, saying it was time to check under the bench.

Curiosity blended with a sudden urge to do as the Viscount demanded, and the need to divert her melancholy. Sadie waited until late afternoon and went looking for the spade.

Chapter 3 Time To Begin Again

The ground was harder than Sadie had imagined. The gardener made it seem so easy to push around the dirt when he had been tending the land. With focused determination, she dragged the solid bench out of the way and carefully removed the grass on top so she could replace the greenery when she was done. Then she dug the hole in earnest. Finally, she found the small box hidden beneath the tree roots, creating their own spidery fingers of protection.

With some work and tenacity, Sadie finally extricated the old wooden strongbox from the tree's grip. Oddly afraid of being discovered now that she held the container, she checked to make sure there was no one witnessing her work. Then she checked in the diminishing light what else there might be buried with the wooden case but found nothing.

She efficiently refilled the hole as quickly as she could. Brushing the dirt from her skirt, she replaced the section of grass on top and pushed the bench over the lot. Finally, she scooped up the small chest and walked resolutely to the library. It seemed fitting that she would open it in that room.

Lighting a candle and being thankful for the heavy greenery creating perfect privacy in the garden, Sadie sighed her relief at reentering the house without being seen. The neighbors continued the pattern of privacy on their properties, each garden like its own little country, separate from the adjoining ones. Sadie sat the box on his lordship's desk gingerly. The weight was immense. Sitting for a moment to dream about what would be inside, she slowly tried to lift the lid. Nailed shut! What was a person to do when there were so many obstacles in her way?

"Anything worth having is worth working for, Sarah Morgan," she chided herself.

When she came back from the kitchen where the cook always kept a few tools, Sadie pried the lid off and stared at the contents. She had never seen such

33

a sight in her life. It was more money than she had ever even imagined touching, and it was hers. Hers to start a new life, become a proper lady, and enjoy the nice things London had to offer. Wait, silly girl. You must count it first.

She laid out the coins uniformly across the desk, stacking denominations of coins to make counting easier. Then she rummaged for a quill, ink, blotter, and parchment. She knew how to pen things and how to count because she had learned all she could from anyone who would teach her. Even without counting it, she knew it was more money than she would ever need to accomplish what she wanted, her independence.

To find an unassuming man who was a good provider. One who didn't want to change her but loved her as she was. Even the part of her that wished, on some days, to do nothing more than return to the time in her life when her cares of today belonged to someone else. This might buy her all of that and more.

When she looked inside the box to ensure she had retrieved all the coins, there was a sealed envelope. With shaking hands, she caressed the familiar seal done in a lighter red, almost pink, which she said she would use as a seal color. It was his reminder of all they shared. Lady Clarise had suggested the seal and Sadie had chosen the pink tint.

"Lighter than his Lordship's seal but close enough to know the connection if they knew the household. Now, let us work on your design. Possibly your first initial with a uniquely designed decoration."

Sadie had been thrilled to engage in such a ladylike activity. It took a few weeks of careful trial and error to decide upon the exact design, incorporating the stylistic "S" and elements of Lady Clarise's intaglio ring. They decided on the initial 'S' because when she married, the second letter would change, and she wanted to use her stamp for a long time. When it arrived several months later on her own ring, Lady Clarise had kept it hidden for Sadie in her writing desk, so no one stole it. Lord Henderson had later moved it to his study. She had used it on her letters to Lord Griffin.

The note in the box said, "Remember we loved you." The handwriting was firm and strong, unlike the gentleman's handwriting before he died. It had gone light and unsure.

It was hard stepping into his study, not only for the scents but because she was rarely invited into its inner sanctum. She much preferred the library for the study was for chastisements, and lessons to be taught and learned. The library exuded comfort.

The scent of his tobacco brought tears to her eyes as she opened the drawer. Lady Clarise would fill his pipe while sitting on her husband's knee. It was something Sadie remembered with fondness. Moving the pouch aside, in search of her ring, Sadie stopped to steady her nerves as she saw another letter, only this one had the familiar handwriting of her benefactor recently. Wanting to prolong reading the last communication she would ever receive from the dear couple, Sadie set the envelope aside to look for the delicate ring stamp.

While Lord Henderson had been kind to her, especially in the years after his wife died, overall, he was a lord who ran his home and business with high expectations, which included the things Sadie should and should not do. It was his way of showing he cared by ensuring she was safe at home and in society once his protection was removed. Sadie knew that if she were truly theirs, she would have had a husband chosen by now. She smiled. They had done more than enough.

Grabbing the ring and placing it on her finger that it now fit perfectly, she swallowed the melancholy and stepped back into the hallway, gently closing the door behind her. She wished she didn't ever have to leave this house. She curled back up into a sofa in the library and opened the envelope carefully.

Dear Sarah,

Lady Clarise and I were never able to have our own children and, as such, have no heirs. While the bulk of the money that we leave behind will go to my brother or his heirs equally, we wanted to ensure your future.

We mourned with you the loss of your dear mother. You were out of the nursery but a long way from adulthood. Please know, after we are gone, that we loved you. Lady Clarise and I have taken you as our own in the only way we could. We kept you close, provided for your needs, and made sure you had as many advantages as we could give you without causing the staff to resent you.

We did many things in secret or behind closed doors. Things like teaching you to read, how to keep books, and understand the rudiments of business so you would not become vulnerable or taken advantage of while you find a fit husband to take over those tasks.

Lady Clarise offered you skills young women need, and while you are no opera singer or astounding artist, you can hold your own in a drawing room. And she taught you her love of good horseflesh. Something I have never been able to appreciate as well as the two of you.

So, it is with great sadness and joy that we leave you with the sum of £5,000. If you wed before we pass from this earth, you will receive this speech and money at your nuptials for your dowry. If you are getting the dowry from the strongbox, then this letter must suffice.

It is a scary amount of money for one yet to be married, if that is when you receive it, but we wanted you to be independent. Spend it well. Our solicitor is expecting you to reach out to him to advise you on housing, employing a savvy housekeeper, an experienced maid, and possibly a footman for as long as you need them. Be frugal and use this opportunity to find a husband worthy of you.

If you choose to stay in the townhouse, let the solicitor know, and he will advise you on the options. There is a map on the back of this paper, and should you stay, I suggest you leave bits of money in each of the hidden places. You are a young lady of some means now, and it is not safe to leave it in a desk where anyone can take it. Destroy this map as a safety precaution.

Stay safe. Live well. All our love to you as you embark on your wonderful future. Your knight in shining armor should arrive shortly.

Remember us fondly,

Lord Henderson and Lady Clarise

The next morning was a stormy day, and the rains were torrential. The tears flowed heavily off and on for the remainder of the evening, Sadie ultimately fell into a fitful sleep until daybreak, and then into a deep, hard sleep for several hours. She decided not to dwell on her botched plans to go to the solicitor today but instead got a bit of bread and marmalade, a pot of strong, hot tea, and planned her future, starting with where she would live.

She carefully wrote out a frugal budget using the pen and paper she did not use the day before. Not so frugal that she couldn't enjoy the world, but she only wished to garner a loyal friend or two and then find her husband. It wasn't that she so much desired a mate, but she needed one in the male-dominated society of London.

And she wouldn't put her money where it could be logged in as money that later would belong to her husband. With such a sum of money, she could care for herself for years. She would live on just the staff money from the will for as much as she could this year, saving all the servants inheritance, and decide what to do after that.

The next day, as she was leaving the house, Sadie didn't hide the fact that she was still in residence. After her visit to the solicitor, she would be the official resident assuming she could rent the home she had always known. It was more overwhelming of an endeavor than she had thought yesterday when she was putting her plan together. It had become much more than being in residence; she had to retain and maintain the same order of life.

Remembering what Lord Henderson had often said, "Today is full of potential, but only if you engage in it," Sadie made sure she started early.

Today, she would do her best to engage and conquer. She checked her appearance and stepped outside. There was a moment of concern that she was not with an escort or a maid, and how unfamiliar that was, but there was nothing for it. She had yet to find someone to fill that spot. She would soon remedy that as well, but today, she would handle it.

Sadie locked the door, something she had never had to do until she was alone. There was another moment of concern for her funds, but she had spent time yesterday distributing them as instructed by Lord Henderson, remembering where each of the five spots were, then she reassured herself that she could breathe easy.

As Sadie stepped out of the door, she inhaled the clear air, warmed by the sun. The rain had reduced most of the unpleasant smells, but if it got much warmer, they would be noticeable. This might be one of the more affluent bits of London, but nature's odors were not to be ignored, both pungent and pleasant.

Not having even a footman to send a message for her was something she had never experienced. Sadie gave herself a final pep talk and headed to the solicitor's office. She had found the address in his lordship's paperwork yesterday. The accounts were very informative. After looking through daily record books, she could see what coal and wood cost in the year, how much the annual tax bill on the townhouse was, and more. Sadie would be sure not to be taken advantage of by tradesmen. As soon as she was able to hire a housekeeper, a maid, and a footman, then she would be set.

As she was entering the office, a man came out looking past her as though she weren't there, his mind full of thoughts. The sun may have been out, but the cold was sharp, and he had his greatcoat, scarf, gloves, and wool hat covering nearly all of his exposed skin. The man with him was similarly dressed and conversing.

Even though they did not notice her, she noticed him. Lord Griffin. He stood as elegantly as she remembered from the last time, he visited her lordship. Her mind stalled her in the outer entranceway as she tried to get control of her heart and her thoughts.

Knowing that the mortification would be supreme if he realized who she was, she sternly told her pounding heart to regain control. His lordship had made it abundantly clear she was not who he wanted as a future wife. He was likely married to another now. A true lady, as it should be. Taking a fortifying breath, she turned one last time and met his glance.

His face wore the expression of a man trying to devise who she was. As though he might know her, but Sadie had her long winter coat on with a hood. With that covering pulled up, it would be impossible to clearly see her face in the cavernous material. Besides, she was several years older and considerably more mature, now. Even her body had further blossomed. She turned to the office door.

Sadie entered the offices of Shackleford and Shackleford. The accommodations were rather scant but clean and the clerk was staid with slicked-back hair and a long thin nose that made her want to smile. But neither the state of the offices nor the severe mannerisms of the clerk would dampen her joy at embarking on her new life.

Mr. Shackleford, senior she presumed, met her with a smile and patted her hand in condolences. "I'm so sorry to hear of your loss, my dear Miss Morgan. I am so happy to finally make your acquaintance. Please join me in a cup of tea while we discuss matters."

"Thank you, Mr. Shackleford. I came as soon as I was able, under the circumstances."

"Yes, yes. I should have called on you, but I was unsure if you had decided to stay in the house or if you had decided to go elsewhere."

The sour clerk brought in the tea and looked at Sadie as though she wasn't worth the effort. His employer must have noticed, for he said, "Mr. Gant, I would not be agreeable to retain your services if you cannot choose to be more accommodating to my clients."

The man mumbled what might have been an apology before quickly exiting the room, closing the door quietly.

"Now, my dear, are you the only one left in the house?"

"Yes, sir. Did Lord Henderson tell you that he left me some funds in addition to the employee severance?"

"He did. Did you bring those funds with you?"

"No. Lord Henderson instructed me on the placement to ensure its safekeeping, and I have done so."

"Ah." The gentleman leaned back in his chair and considered her for a moment. Sadie returned his gaze steadily. "Well, if you ever need me to help you in that regard, I am at your service. I have sent the communication to the gentleman that Lord Henderson instructed me to do, so all the old business is complete."

"To whom did you send the letter?"

The older man shook his head. "Lord Henderson instructed me on matters as well. I cannot tell you."

"What was written?"

The man shook his head. "I do not know, for I did not unseal it. Lord Henderson sealed it himself, but I believe the gentleman to be a very safe man. My dealings with him have been most agreeable. Now then, what do we need to accomplish today?"

Sadie sat and stared at Mr. Shackleford, taking a sip of tea and setting the cup down with measured movements. Deciding it was a waste of breath to discuss the identity of the gentleman further, she continued in a new direction.

"Right. I have perused the accounts and notes left by my benefactor. I would like to continue renting the townhouse if that is possible."

"Did he not tell you? Lord Henderson owned the house on Grosvenor."

"Owned? So does that mean it goes to his brother?"

"No. The family estate that Lord Henderson's brother lives in is his, but not the London house."

"I thought he owned the townhouse, but I saw him log in a number for a rental amount every month."

"Ah, yes. He did own another townhouse and received rents from it, not the one he lived in."

Her shoulders sagged a bit with disappointment. "Then I suppose we must find me a place to live."

"Do you wish me to dispose of the house for you?"

"For me?" she felt her forehead crease, and she relaxed her face to avoid wrinkles. "I'm sorry. I am more affected by the circumstances than I had thought. Could you explain the situation again, sir?"

"It is yours. Well, to make it legally binding, you must purchase it from the estate for the sum of one pound."

"It's... I'm sorry. I want to make sure I understand. He left me the house if I purchase it for one pound. The house that I presently live in. The home I have always lived in with Lord and Lady Henderson?"

Chapter 4 Time To Reassess

Mr. Shackleford gave a look of confused amusement. "That is what his will states and what he instructed me to tell you. I have the deed to present to you. May I ask your wishes?"

Sadie fished around in her reticule and pulled out a pound coin she had expected to need to use to help secure the home but not purchase it.

"I am staying, Mr. Shackleford. So, I suppose I need you to assist me in procuring help, and whatever else is needed. I do know how to pay the coal and food bills and so on. His lordship taught me a great many things on that score. He said I may need the knowledge sometime in the future, but I had not understood just what he meant. I am now surmising the sum of all he wanted me to understand and the reasoning behind it."

"Indeed," said the older gentleman.

It was obvious to Sadie that he did not approve of young ladies having any knowledge of such things and possibly not even owning houses. Certainly he would have something to say about her staying there without a male protector.

"I have a frugal budget in preparation."

"Let us discuss what you will need and the annual cost. I am sure you will find a suitable husband soon to relieve you of the burden."

Sadie decided not to respond as she would have wished to the last remark. She had only thought of one man as her ultimate spouse and since he was no longer in the offing, she was not eager to fill the vacancy. She decided to answer his first statement.

"Yes, I would like that. If you wouldn't mind, please come to the house when you have applicants, hopefully within the week, and we shall interview them together."

The older man was not expecting that kind of invitation. He seemed to not be sure if he was flattered or insulted. "Yes, of course."

"I should be thankful. I cannot be in society often without an escort; therefore, a maid is my most immediate need. After that, we shall need a cook/housekeeper and a footman at the very least. A gardener on the occasion would be nice, I suppose, but again, not an immediate need. It is still winter."

The man was writing things down and then leaned back in his chair as if he had just finished a large meal. "Is there anything else of immediate need?"

"I know Lord Henderson had no less than nine employees, and often eleven, but I require three immediately. The rest I will decide upon as I discuss things with my housekeeper." She stood. "And if you will introduce me to the tradesmen that Lord Henderson had, it will be easier to continue service with them."

"Yes, I will take care of that."

"Thank you. I must take my leave, there are so many little things to take care of."

Sadie just wanted to go home. The thought of Lord Henderson being truly dead had hit her again. She stood, hoping for a quick exit before her tears reappeared.

"Madam, I will send Mr. Gant. He is, at least, an escort."

"Do you not feel it would be unseemly if a man, not of my acquaintance, accompanied me on my errands?"

He frowned. "Then let me send for one of my maids."

"Thank you, but by the time she arrives, I may well have finished my errands and find myself at home sipping tea. This is the only time I am inconvenienced. Please do not concern yourself. I will see you before week's end."

Being a lady was exhausting. This was one of those carefree times she wished she could allow someone else, a husband perhaps, to take care of everything. Sadie stood, took the will, the bill of sale, the old deed, and the one with her name on it. She also accepted several other bits of paperwork and with a smile she didn't feel, she left.

As she stepped out of the offices of Mr. Shackleford, she saw that snow had fallen and so had the temperatures. Not seeing a hack, she brought up the hood of Lady Clarise's heavy long coat, now hers, and tied her knitted scarf, also from her late mistress, and rushed out into the street where she ran into an immovable object.

"Oh, I am so sorry, sir. Please forgive me."

Sadie's attempted smile froze before it was fully formed. Lord Griffin. Again. How could it be that she had literally walked into him after walking past him not one hour ago? The lord who would be a duke. The Duke of Amesbury now, she supposed, since Lord Henderson had told her of the recent death of Lord Griffin's father. Richard's letter later confirmed it. He had a black armband. He was in mourning.

Sadie quickly looked away, but not before she caught a glimpse of an even more attractive man than she had remembered as a visitor in what was now her home. He appeared to be puzzled, likely still thinking he recognized her and yet could not place her. She was underage when he met her, and they had not spent a long time together before he left and the multiple family losses between them had necessitated any furthering of their acquaintance be put on hold.

Spying, yes, she had taken to doing just as he had accused her of in jest, that introductory evening. She was nothing he would have taken an interest in if he had been looking for a wife then. She had entertained him in the interim, but things must have truly changed. She hadn't thought she had altered at all but seeing the maturity in him, she must have done some of her own. It mattered not, now, for he was probably married.

"Are you hurt, milady?" came the deep, resonating voice of the man in her dreams.

"I am not. I apologize profusely. It was irresponsible of me to not watch the direction I was turning into."

She had to get away before he discovered who she was. Why? She did not know, but she did not want to find out.

"Nonsense. I am glad you are well." He looked around and his tone changed to one of reproof. "Where is your maid, madam?"

"She is in the shops. I'm on my way to find her now that my errand is complete. Thank you for inquiring. I bid you good day, sir."

"Wait."

Sadie rushed off before any more words could be spoken, and he discovered who she was. Somehow, she knew he would not allow her to go anywhere unaccompanied and would have a considerable amount to say about it. She felt embarrassed to see him after she had dreamed of him so often. It wasn't as though she had dominion over her dreams, but they now caused her to experience humiliation, nonetheless.

He did not return as he had predicted in the last letter he sent. She was of marriageable age, and that made any communication more serious, indeed. It had become clear he didn't wish to pursue that line of thinking. Better not to encourage such imaginings of a man out of her reach. Sadie rushed down the slushy streets and found a hack to hire. Better to ride today than walk. She was too out of sorts now to take care not to fall.

Over the next week, while colder than she remembered was typical, she went to the market and several other places for the needed items. As she passed Lord Henderson's club, she felt eyes on her. She glanced over and found the afternoon sun created a glare in the glass, preventing her from seeing in. She stood for a few moments, but when she had to dodge an odious man's attentions, she left.

But the feeling didn't go away the next time she went past and this time she saw her Lord Duke inside, looking out with several other gentlemen. She peered in, now hoping for him to recognize her but she must have been too wrapped in her winter wear. Or he was married already. She continued on her way and took a different street home partly because she didn't want to be discovered and because the obnoxious man who seemed to be on the corner daily was beginning to harass her again.

A message was delivered on Thursday for Friday. The applicants were to come for interviews, but Mr. Shackleford sent his apologies for not being able to attend. He had other clients and work he needed to complete. He sent his regrets.

"Regrets?" she asked out loud to an empty house. "Cowardliness more like."

Sadie's confidence flagged. She was fearful to do this alone. The mere presence of another person would be a confidence builder. "You know what a good person looks and sounds like, Sadie. And you certainly can spot a lazy person," she told the empty room. "I will be fine."

She would have to do these things for herself from now on, so she might as well start now. She wondered what attributes the duke would expect in his employees. Of course, except for estate managers and the like, he would never have hired others. It was a task for those who oversaw things to do. Since she thought of Richard, had seen him, her meanderings went further and now she would never get the man out of her thoughts or dreams.

The next day, when the first applicants arrived, she was prepared. She would be done by teatime, so Sadie had the tea tray set, the kettle ready to boil on the kitchen stove, and a bit of meat and bread and fruit cake she found in the basement larder.

She wasn't likely to have help for tonight and cooking was never something she had mastered. Soups and small bits of roasted meats were almost all she could do. She was ready for something else. Sadie was never so glad as now that she had taken her lessons on how to run a household seriously because it was a lifeline she intended to use.

By the end of the afternoon, she had hired a whole family who had just lost their positions in their old home due to the mistress remarrying and moving to Scotland. Mr. and Mrs. Flander, their two sons and two daughters were the last to be interviewed. Mrs. Flander interviewed for housekeeper, and she mentioned that her husband and children, aged sixteen, seventeen, eighteen, and nineteen were with her as well.

Intrigued, she had them in the room by the time it was all said and done. The others who had been interviewed were disappointing candidates, to say the least, and while she had only wanted three employees to start, she did love the way Mrs. Flander and Mr. Flander were with her, each other, and their offspring.

"I'm not sure what to say. I had not intended to have so many staff this soon."

"You have a large home."

"I do, but I won't have many visitors, so I intend to live simply this winter. Meaning, I don't intend to open the extra bedrooms save my room and one guest room, which is important to keep at the ready."

Mr. Flander spoke, his voice firm and yet very kind. "Having room and board this winter is quite enough, milady. We would be happy to take the income for three this winter if you would be willing to take us all."

"Oh, but that would not be fair. I intended on hiring a housekeeper, maid, and footman until spring. But I have to say that having a butler to take care of those duties and help ensure the security of the household does sound appealing. So, I will pay full wages for those four positions and the other two will work for room and board only. Only until spring. I shall want a personal maid at that time and another footman, so wages will begin in May."

She settled the price using the guidelines the viscount had taught her.

Mrs. Flander's tears were joined by her daughters' and if Sadie stared hard, she believed her new butler sported water in the eye as well. It was winter and if the others needed work as much as the Flanders, then Sadie didn't think it right not to compensate the applicants for their time. She sent each away with a penny and her appreciation for answering the ad.

"Milady, you shouldn't have. It isn't done."

"Yes, I know, but it is winter, and I have been the recipient of much kindness in my life. It is important I pay that forward. Now, Mrs. Flander, can Mr. Flander and your sons gather your belongings? Then I will show you to the kitchen and if you would be so kind as to finish preparing my tea, I would be happy for you to acquaint yourself with the house today. Your quarters are on the third floor this winter. We shall start work in earnest tomorrow."

Sadie didn't correct the new staff on addressing her as my lady. It was fitting, and they seemed comfortable with it, so she let it be. Now, she first needed to remember the staff's names and then invest small bits of funds as Lord Henderson taught her and begin learning how to live as a woman of means.

But as the days yawned into weeks and then a month, now two, Sadie knew she had made a grave error in judgment. A mistake she didn't know how to undo.

Chapter 5 Time For Adjustments

Richard watched her from the window and continued to be mesmerized by her beauty of spirit. Richard had thought that the young woman was a mere girl who was still enamored with life. Her exuberance and engaging smile seemed as yet unfettered by the burdens of the adult world and reminded him of those carefree days of his youth. There was something very familiar about the girl, but he couldn't recall why.

Was she the girl saw her for several days and then nothing. Instead of being relieved that she was not out and about, Richard became concerned after the second day of not laying eyes on her. It was after the third day of perusing that the young lady returned, possibly due to living nearby. There was something about her that always brought Sarah to mind.

Now, full on winter, Richard saw her around the corner of the block. It was then, as he watched the sway of her ample qualities that he discovered she wasn't a mere girl, but a woman. Slight, but with definite traits of a lady, he watched her differently now. His mother may despair of the revealing nature of dress in these times, but at this moment, Richard could see nothing but benefit.

She was young, yes, but a grown woman nonetheless, for no child had those hips that swayed in the day's breeze, shifting the form-fitting gown nor lush breasts of that magnitude. His pantaloons tightened, and he was glad for the ample walnut table and long draping cloth that covered its top and his lower half. He knew this woman, but he could not place her. He would recall her.

The members of this club were often of impeccable heritage and upbringing, wealthy, and distinctly comfortable being the master of not only their homes but of their destinies. They also enjoyed being masters in their marriages to wives they would easily die for.

Many men of his caliber were seen as heartless and cruel to their families and households. Inconsiderate of their fellow man and self-centered was the rule of the day. Indeed, they were, but in the circles that Richard socialized, the men were loving and cherished their wives and family above all else.

Protective and possessive, their type of marriage might not fit the women who want to live their lives separate from their husbands. The marriage Richard expected would place him at the head but with an ear to his wife's desires.

He sighed. He wanted to stop the young woman and chastise her for being without an escort and mostly because she reminded him of another young woman. Where was his Sadie? He had checked around and even gone to Henderson House where he had hoped she'd still be but no answer. He tried to locate the butler and his wife to no avail. Richard was devastated.

He looked back out the window. What must she be thinking? His protective instincts skyrocketed, and his hand itched with the need to punish naughtiness. Like his Sadie, the young woman wouldn't like it, but, also like his Sadie, she would understand it and submit. Then he would take her to the heights of pleasure for her acceptance. Sadie, he wanted her so badly.

He renewed his determination to claim her soon. Sadie. She attracted him like no other. She drew him as the proverbial moth to the flame. It was a certain knowledge deep in his chest, in the core of his being. He needed to possess her. Sadie. Richard took one last look at the young girl before turning away to listen to his friends discuss the next business venture consideration. But he kept one eye on her as she spoke to the man on the street.

His friend, Lord Kendrick, mentioned her after a few minutes. "Is she lost?"

Evidently, all at the table had eyes on her for no one asked who he was referring to.

"I have seen her a few times these last days, but never before. I don't believe she is."

"Where is her escort?" asked another friend. Lord Thayer's tone was severe.

"Or her father to allow such behavior?" asked his friend Lord Ashton.

"Certainly, she has no papa," said Richard. Jasper remained quiet. The others murmured agreement.

For the rest of the evening, every time he thought of the young woman long gone from the corner, he felt a tendril of concern for her safety and each time assured himself that he was likely mistaken. She was fine. His attraction was because of his constant thought of a wife. His young Sadie.

When they left the club, it was later than usual and, as on all other days, he watched the corner and the adjoining streets to see if there was a glimpse of her. Richard was staying with Jasper as the man spent most of his time in London and was well-situated. Their friend, Lord Trenton, was in town to rent a house for the spring and early summer so his wife could reacquaint herself with friends she could not enjoy the rest of the year. He was to stay with Jasper as well.

"You've noticed the young lady, I see. I had my eye on her, but she isn't an abbess or anything close. Wouldn't you agree? There is just something enticing about her," said Jasper.

"She's a Darling."

"Is she? How do you know?" Jasper was his closest friend but the feeling of jealousy, even anger was something that came unbidden, and Richard immediately squelched it.

Richard shrugged. "One can tell. I've noticed her and watched her. I am confident in stating she is a Darling albeit a naughty one for exposing herself unescorted."

"Yes, it's the unescorted bit that made me believe she is one for adventures. But now, I see, she had gone from the corner. She could have had a liaison."

"No, I am confident that she is a Darling and an innocent."

"Maybe she knows the quiet reputation of this club, and is looking for an escort within these walls," said Jasper with a shrug.

Jasper seemed to not concern himself with her any longer. Richard was relieved. Of course, she was gone. It was getting bloody cold to join this rain. Not for the first time this week did he wonder why he came to London in the lingering winter. He was still in mourning but there was business he had to complete. He had one final thought as to if the young woman was home in front of a warming fire or trying to find her way there?

That thought worried him almost as much as the fact that he had seen her several times unaccompanied. Again, the unbidden thought of what was Sadie doing crossed his mind and took up residence there. Lord Henderson had stalled Richard's attempts to talk to him about Sadie and now that he was finishing his year of mourning soon, he would push the issue.

He was going to return in a few months, and he would never wonder what she was doing again. He was determined to make Lady Sarah his.

SADIE'S STAFF SO EFFECTIVELY met all her needs that she rarely left the house. Unfortunately, due to her change of circumstances, she rarely had a visitor and even those were more likely to be tradesmen or the modiste. That was fine in the cold, but as the weather lightened and warming breezes began to arrive, the Flanders' behavior never changed. They rarely allowed her to go anywhere, always choosing to go themselves.

She found it suspicious that they didn't even want her to go to the solicitors herself. Exerting her newfound freedom was difficult but not impossible. Sadie's concerns grew.

Fearing to keep any valuables, money, or papers in her home, she gathered what she could and walked out into the garden, slipped through the hedge she had watched a young maid slip through last year, and got a hack from the street. She didn't explain to her staff where she had been and for what purpose, and the air became very stilted. Something had to be done.

Sadie refused the assistance almost forced on her each time she chose to leave and after coming and going with no help, she could finally exit the house alone with a little ingenuity. Sadie knew it was important to go with an escort, but she couldn't take one of the girls with her, for they were very disrespectful, and it was tiring and vexing.

She brought her concerns to the solicitor, and on the third visit, chose to have a message delivered to her friends Mr. and Mrs. Arnold by courier through the solicitor. Sadie had begun to wonder if she was receiving all her correspondence and was relieved when the Arnolds arrived on their first day off without sending notice. Sadie wouldn't have put it past Mr. Flander to make her unavailable.

As luck would have it, Sadie was passing the entrance and answered the knock of her dear friends, it was clear the Flanders were not best pleased that Sadie had visitors, but the immediate lessening of her fears was immense.

"Shall we go for a walk, my dear?" asked Mrs. Arnold. "Mr. Arnold will stay behind and follow up on the way the household is run. If you don't mind, of course. He has a way about him. Nothing will get by him, and he won't allow it to, either." The woman was so confident, Sadie felt no problem leaving him there.

"I'm afraid to be alone with them, Mrs. Arnold. What have I done?"

"You've fallen for an old trick, my dear and if you were to have told us your plans, Mr. Arnold and I would have stayed on for you." The older woman tsked.

"I didn't know until you were settled in your new home. And I am positive all my correspondence is not arriving or being sent properly."

"Never you mind, my girl. All will be right now."

Relieved this wasn't her ineptitude in running a house or understanding the way of staff as the lady of the house, she sighed. "Thank you for telling me that. But now, dear woman, what am I to do?"

"Why, dismiss them at once."

"Can I do that? What if they refuse?"

"Oh yes, this is a fine time to dismiss staff. There are many positions open, although I suspect they are not typical staff. They look for the vulnerable."

Sadie digested this bit of good news and then furrowed her brow again. "And how am I ever going to hire again? I failed so miserably this time."

"Mr. Arnold and I will interview with you. It isn't such a task but never stay in a house alone with people you've never met before and aren't trusting. It is a woefully hard world out there, my dear. Now, tell me the entire story of how we got to today."

The women talked for several hours, stopping to have a treat in a local pub.

"I just want someone to take care of the onerous tasks like this and yet allow me to be my own person. I know it sounds odd, but is there a way that I can have only a child's responsibilities at times and a woman's duties on all other occasions?"

Mrs. Arnold smiled and nodded. "It isn't a subject we can discuss here, but yes, that is possible with the right husband."

"I need to find where that husband might be. How do I find him, for I cannot experience this grave error of judgment again."

"No, indeed you cannot."

The women grabbed a hack and rode it to a club and on the ride, Mrs. Arnold explained the little she knew about such things as papas and Lord Henderson's care of Lady Henderson.

"But she was not a woman who needed assistance in caring for her home." Richard referred to himself as a papa. This is what he meant. It must be.

"Indeed, not. But she did have a side that only his lordship knew about and whom she relied on him to take care of."

"I believe I remember several such incidents that I was within earshot of. I thought it odd, but so comforting. Lord Griffin, umm, the Duke of Amesbury, is one such person, I believe."

"Not every woman wants that, mind. Many of us do not. But for those who do, it is incredible to have your needs met. But be careful because not only are you cuddled, but you are also chastised when you make the wrong decision."

Sadie nodded and hoped her face didn't turn red as she felt the heat rise and reach deep into her lower regions at the thought of being kissed and chastised. Richard had spoken of such things and had indeed done both already.

She could only imagine what it felt like to be kissed, but she had been thrashed a time or two and while it was not pleasant, thinking about her husband doing the punishing somehow made it exciting. With Richard as her husband, the ache returned to full force.

"Where is this place, Mrs. Arnold? We need to get back soon."

"We do. Here, at this corner. It is a club known to draw men who enjoy being papas to women. Either mistresses or wives. Possibly other, more unsavory instances as well, but we shan't bother with those."

The hack stopped and both women looked out the window.

"I have passed this corner several times and never knew it was more than a gentlemen's club for ordinary men. I believe Richard, the duke, frequents here. You say there are men of this same ilk, papa? Do I knock on the door and beg entrance?"

"Heavens no. That would ruin you. No, do you remember the men that you met, several years ago?"

"Yes, before Lady Clarise died. I remember. There was one..."

"One who caught your eye? Lady Clarise said as much. What is his name? It is the lord who would be a duke, I believe you called him? Yes, that is Richard. But I believe he is no longer interested in me. I have not had any correspondence from him in months."

"Or his correspondence was hidden? Disposed of?"

Sadie moaned her understanding. "Yes. I'm sure it was. But now, it doesn't matter, does it? He is not interested in me, and he is likely married by now. I mean, why wouldn't he be? A lord who would be duke someday has responsibilities."

Mrs. Arnold nodded. "He is a duke now, I hear. Her ladyship thought as much. He rents not far from you during the spring and early summer seasons. And according to gossip, is quite an eligible bachelor with more money than he can count."

The hack pulled up to the house and when Sadie instructed him to wait for a final fare, she withheld the fee.

"I'll bring out your fare when I return."

She had seen his lordship do that once, and it had worked like a charm.

"If I pay him now, he might go off with the next fare and I would have to make do. I like to know the outcome when I can." Sadie understood that sentiment only too well having learned to be self-preserving in recent weeks.

When Mr. Arnold met them at the door, Sadie crinkled her brow, expecting Mr. Flander. There was no one peeking around the corner, no one looking down the staircase. No one at all.

"Mr. Arnold, where is everyone? Are you alone?" Sadie knew that wasn't possible, for she had rarely entered a room in the last weeks that someone wasn't dogging her heels.

"Yes, my dear. We are quite alone."

"But..."

"The Flanders thought it was time to look for other employment. Winter is well and truly over, and the prospects being many, now was the perfect time to find another residence. I suggested the large country estates, and they agreed."

"I may be naïve, Mr. Arnold, but I know better than that. Might they have made that decision based on your encouragement?"

He smiled but said nothing in return. "I will send back one of the savvier maids for you to keep with you until we find appropriate staff."

"But your employer..."

"Won't even notice as he is out of the country for another few weeks. She won't be missed."

"I don't know how to thank you both."

"I'm sure Mrs. Arnold discussed the poor choice of not informing us of your circumstances."

He sounded just like she expected a father to sound when he was less than enthused over his offspring's choice. And raised his brow as a father in chastising mode but more formal.

"Yes, and I do apologize for my actions. Do you forgive my error in judgment?"

"There is nothing to forgive, but if there were, you would be forgiven, dear girl. Now, we must get back, so you are not alone too far into the evening. Answer only to the maid's knock. She will say Lilliputian when she begs entrance."

"Oh, yes? Well, I shall be on the lookout for the secret word. Why, exactly do we need one?"

"I don't trust the Flanders to not send someone in their stead to try to gain entrance."

"Oh, I didn't pay them for this week."

"You mean month?"

"Oh, no. They asked for weekly as they were used to that payment arrangement."

"I assure you they were not." Mr. Arnold stated strongly. "And they have helped themselves to a few bits and bobs during their sojourn here. Not much, but some I found in their rooms and on their persons before they left. I divested them of what they were leaving with and told them that should they return; you would report them for theft. All of them. Seems they didn't need much when they left."

"We must go, Mr. Arnold."

"Yes, Mrs. Arnold."

Mrs. Arnold hugged Sadie, and he patted her shoulder as she gave them the fare. They protested, but Sadie was adamant. They promised to send the maid and contact her within the week with staff possibilities.

Once they were gone, the place felt scary and empty. Not yet dark, but even though Mr. Arnold promised he had gone through the entire house locking doors and windows, Sadie was worried they would return and exact their revenge, so she checked all again. Mr. Arnold said they weren't even all family. He had heard of this Flander group from other staff. They preyed on the vulnerable. Sadie hated she was considered vulnerable, but the truth of it was she had been an easy mark, for sure.

She wished for a man who took care of her, so she didn't have to worry about such things. Not tell her what to do but keep things safe. The man that came to her mind, immediately, was the duke. She wished he would come and visit her but, it was the wrong season and while she had seen him some months ago, she was sure he was gone from London. Winter wasn't a time to be galivanting around London.

Once the maid came, Sadie locked herself in the library and cried herself to sleep. She wondered when the duke would return to London. She determined to find out if his feelings had waned.

Chapter 6 Time For Change

Winter had been longer than expected, but now the world was beginning to wake up, and Richard finally allowed himself to acknowledge that he was ready not to dodge the leg shackling his friends had succumbed to. All but Jasper that was. He wasn't going to be the elusive buck that was many young women's prey. And that thought always brought him to the woman who he had set his eyes on. Would she feel like he was homing in on her as his most desirous prey? She'd be right. He would settle for no one else but Sadie. He was ready to address the fact that his letters had not been responded to.

Richard Anthony Griffin had officially become the Duke of Amesbury at twenty-seven, but even when his father was still living, most had referred to him as Your Grace. When alone and in an affectionate mood, his sister still referred to him as Griff, for he had a close affinity with her. But he was the duke now and he wondered if their sibling closeness would continue after he married, and she did the same. Life was about to change for both of them.

"It has been thirteen months since your father passed, Richard. I would that you now consider taking a wife. My widow weeds are dispensed, and I believe I might take a gander at the parties for myself," said the duchess.

What his mother didn't know was that he had offered for the only woman he wanted as a wife, his Darling Duchess, and she had not responded. Nor had Lord Henderson, her benefactor. He didn't technically have to ask Henderson, but he was a friend and he had taken Sadie under his wing, so it was only proper to do so. Neither, however, had communicated with a return message. Resulting in the last few months becoming a churning battle with his emotions.

For the hundredth time since his conversation with his mother and sister about finding a wife and the need for a husband for Julia, young Sarah came to mind. It was also not the first time this week that he thought about his age and that it was time to seek out Sarah. Was it time to begin that part of his life? Yes.

And according to some of his friends, he'd left it off a bit long. Sarah would be how old now? Twenty or twenty-one, and that was old enough to decide if she was ready to take up a life with him.

Although he was very good at what he did on the estate and the family businesses, he didn't have complete confidence in his ability to be a good husband and father. After all, his example was not a good one. Nevertheless, it was time he expanded his horizons and met the final bit of his family responsibilities. He was eager to see if she was truly the *Darling* he suspected she was. When he had mentioned chastisement, she had responded beautifully.

Being a man of obligation for most of his adult life, it was now second nature to consider what was required of him before doing what he wanted to do. Richard was in an excellent position and could choose his activities on any day, but he'd often been called a workhorse rather than an engaging friend. He would have to change those traits if Sadie was the woman for him. He would have additional parts to play. The role of husband and papa to his Darling Duchess.

What he needed was to find a balance between running the new businesses and the old estate responsibilities that his father left with him once he left Richard's mother. The older Duke never had much of a business acuity, nor did he have insight as to how to run the estate, efficiently. That would include caring for a family.

In Richard's estimation, what he needed was to settle down and turn over the running of the household and personnel and the social obligations to a woman. And while he would love to say that he could choose a good woman to substitute hostess for him, without marriage that was unlikely to happen, even if he were so inclined.

Unfortunately taking on a wife expanded his responsibilities tangibly. He not only would be expected to attend to his wife and would give way to births and social engagements, he would have to be host to others more often. The only activity that he had historically looked forward to, was the one that would produce offspring. However, if he got the woman he wanted, Sarah, there would be much more than congress and hosting others in their marriage. His own Little Lady... he smiled. His Darling Duchess. Sarah would be up to the task of being a duchess.

While waiting for a return response to his letter, Richard had grown restless, then irritated and angry, and now his feelings of hurt had made way for sadness and grumpiness. His mother bringing up the very subject that made him so touchy caused him to force the reality of his situation to light. Why had they not given him the courtesy of a response? Something must have happened to one or both of them.

His thoughts returned to the fears he had nearly a month ago. Had she married? Or maybe they had sent a reply and it had gone by the wayside as these missives sometimes did from London to the country. Or, he had been rejected. This time. Richard was known for his daring business moves, and there was no reason he should change his ways when procuring a wife. But he didn't just want any woman, he wanted Sadie. It was time to go and find out just where the issue lie.

His mother, Lady Margaret was speaking to him, and, out of respect for her, he refocused his thoughts from Sadie and his abject failure in that department to his mother. His planning would have to wait a little longer.

"Excuse me, I didn't hear you Mother." He had, but it explained the gap in response.

"No, you don't often hear anyone these days. I think that is a great indicator that you need a wife, dear. Something to divert your efforts and draw your attention to. Someone to help you refocus on the life around you. It's time, Richard."

"Am I to understand that you have put me on notice?" He forced his face to show a smile.

"Of a kind. Your sister is desirous of her own home. When that happens, my duty will be accomplished, and I find I am in want of companionship."

"Mother, I did not know your present companion was not meeting your needs. You have but to ask and I would find you a score of companions."

"A score?" she laughed. "My dear, I don't require more than the one I have. The male variety was what I was speaking of. I have gone too long without it. I wouldn't need to take her with me at all, which she would be happy with, should I find a suitable gentleman to keep company with, but I am not without emotional resources."

Richard laughed. "Women never are. Take care that your suitable gentleman is one with his own fortune."

Richard knew his mother had been the long-suffering wife while her husband made no bones about the fact that he desired and lived with his mistress. Richard would ensure the upkeep of his mother but not her love interest.

"Never fear. Should that gentleman ever present, I promise he will be one who can not only keep me in my accustomed manner of life, but he will also be able to exceed it."

"Ah. Then do you have the same high hopes for my sister?"

"To be sure. But you must decide what you will settle on her."

The duke turned to examine his mother and then the room for a moment as if to calm himself. His outrage was barely suppressed.

"Of course she will have her dowry, but are you saying that without a trail of coin to follow Julia, there will not be a suitable gentleman interested in my sister?"

Julia was graceful and could carry herself as relaxed or as commanding as a situation demanded, but she was average to gaze upon. Pretty, but not awe-inspiring. For her family and friends, it was of no consequence. She was well loved, and to be sure, her entirety of person was immensely enticing as the line-up of enamored young men in the last year would attest, but she would never be one of England's great beauties.

"Of course not," said Julia at the threshold of the library. "You have always been too protective. That isn't what mother means. I know that I am not what every man envisions for his wife. I am loudly opinionated, but often right, which does not endear me to many of the male variety." She laughed. "There are likely to be no poems written about my unsurpassed beauty, but that is a blessing, is it not?" Her eyes sparkled. "The dowry will be my money, brother, not a bribe."

"Julia." He kissed his sister's cheek as he escorted her further into the room. "Your personality is unsurpassed." countered Richard as he handed her off to sit on the settee. "I didn't mean to sound as though I begrudged your dowry. Indeed, I do not. But I will approve only those who do not have an eye on it. There are men who are confident in their abilities and will not be intimidated by your intelligence or the size of your marriage money."

"That is certainly true." Julia accepted the teacup from her mother. "There are many men cut from the same cloth as you, who my lack of glowing beauty or my nurtured increase of intelligence and opinion will not put off. But I will need bait to get the second or third glance and that is what the dowry is for."

"Indeed. I shan't give a moment's glance to anyone who is not of the highest standards," replied Lady Margaret. "Do not fear you will be left adrift, my dear."

"Nor shall I," said Julia. "But I am more worried about our duke. He is out of mourning and yet, I find no smile. Who have you observed that might meet your standards, brother?"

He laughed. "I believe I have my hands full of women's needs at the moment. When my duty is done, I'll turn inward."

Julia turned to her mother. "You have told him, then."

Lady Margaret nodded. "I thought it was time to inform him of my desire to look around and see what society offers me in my dotage."

Richard's laughter bounced off the book-laden walls. "Dotage? Doing it up a bit strong, aren't you? Exaggeration does not become you. I know of no other matron that ages more gracefully than you, Mother."

"Thank you, dear. It will make the perusing easier. Now, I must leave you because there is so much more to do today."

"And I plan to visit the Carrollton sisters today." Julia gave her brother a mischievous smile as she stood. "Care to come along, Richard? I am sure the ladies would be thrilled."

His response was a grimace. "I am sure you are correct, sister, but thankfully I have plenty of work to occupy me before I take my trip to London."

"Try to get the house on Grosvenor's, dear. We are always most comfortable there."

"I will do my best, Mother." He leaned down to kiss his mother's cheek and then his sister's. "We want to have an appropriate place for all of Julia's gentlemen callers, and if you are serious, Mother, for your callers as well. We must be at our best."

Julia's cheeks heated, and she shook her head as she continued out of the room talking about dukes and their hopes for a duchess.

"Don't distress your sister, Richard. And what of you? Will you look this season for a duchess? Do not let your sister's gazing stop yours."

"I will consider it."

Richard enjoyed women, and he had been known to spend a random night with Mrs. Brown, not likely her honest Christian name, but it didn't matter. He didn't go into having a mistress as he felt it was a waste of money when he could find a wife and dispense with the worry of disease. Many married men continued to visit their evening flower but it was likely Sarah would protest and why would he want to go elsewhere if he had Sarah in his bed?

For the last few years, he had rarely used the services of any lady of the evening, even Mrs. Brown. It just wasn't his style and besides, he couldn't stop thinking of how many other men had sought the favors of the same woman. Mrs. Brown was discreet and selective, but the thought was sometimes more than he could stomach, so he kept to himself as far as dalliances were concerned. And then there was Sadie. He dreamed of her often and had to withhold his greatest desire to arrive in London and simply kidnap her. But, of course, he would never do that.

Finding a woman to call his duchess was more complex than it might sound. He wanted what many men would not require. Some years ago, when he attended Oxford for a short time, he was introduced to many of the men he now called friends. Their preferences in business and private lives were similar.

These men introduced the young Lord Griffin to many pleasurable pastimes of the day, such as excessive drinking and pranking. Those all fell away when he left school to take on more responsibilities at home. The one thing he should have left behind was his plan of someday taking care of his Darling Duchess. Now that the time had come, he found himself hesitant and excited.

The duchess lingered a little longer to explore her son's thoughts.

"Have you someone in mind, my dear?"

"I might be harder to settle than both of you. I find I have exacting tastes, but yes, I believe I do."

"Indeed. Discernment in finding the right woman who would bear and raise your children is not a small endeavor but one I am sure you are more than ready to embark on. Time to go on the hunt. Don't fret so, Richard. It is like a business transaction of which you are well versed."

"I hope you are right. I sincerely hope you are right."

He feared, however, that the truth was further from easy as it could be. He often found young ladies or their mamas watching him as he strolled through their village or town or at sporting events. But it wasn't any of them he wanted. He wanted to pursue only Sadie. It was she on whom he had to concentrate all his efforts.

In University, finding a partner at dances was never a task, but Richard discovered what he truly desired when he went to the home of a woman, easily five years his senior, but who looked younger. She could prove, by baptism papers, that she was indeed older which calmed his mind that she was not some farmer's daughter out for a random adventure.

Penelope had her own rooms in the village, and she had made herself and her knowledge available to several of Richard's friends, so when he approached her one evening in the pub's alcove, she informed him she had specific needs.

"I want you to pretend to be my papa for tonight."

"Pardon me? Madam, I am no one's father."

"Ah, you have yet to discover the wonders of it. Let me show you."

He was shocked at the woman's forwardness, but being in his cups, his pride and inhibitions lowered, he agreed. The woman smiled and then led him into her home. He bumbled around for a few moments before she took charge and directed his actions. Penelope explained how to spank her, kiss her, cuddle her, and how to provide all manner of other delights.

Richard visited her several more times, completely sober, and discovered what he liked. He decided from that time forward that he wanted extra in his bedchamber and in his relationship with his wife when he got one. There was a satisfaction in protecting what was yours and to discipline in a loving but fun way that excited the sexual experience. He learned how to please a sassy woman and how to take command of the situation lovingly when her mischievousness went over the line of his tolerance.

He would please her in a way he had never thought to do. In turn, he learned what he liked. Richard desired a woman who wanted his brand of loving. Loving that he had, over the years with the help of Penelope and later Mrs. Brown, expanded and perfected, especially the papa role. It helped that when he entered the room, he naturally commanded it already, filling it both by stature and by presence.

Young Sarah had noticed it and while not mature enough when he had first met her to marry a duke, she was definitely a Darling. And now, of the right age.

Last night, when Richard escorted his sister and mother to a community gathering, the moment he stepped into the room, the conversation quieted. Many women turned in his direction, but most looked down and then turned away when encountering the intensity of his stare. That isn't what he wanted in a wife. He wanted one who could take care of herself but would allow him to do so when necessary. Someone who would meet his stare fearlessly.

His mind went back to Sarah. They had been approaching an understanding when Lady Clarise died, then his father, and now, if gossip were to be believed, Lord Henderson had just passed. He had yet to get the gossip confirmed from one he considered a reliable source but until then, he operated under the impression that Lord Henderson was gone. What did that mean for Sadie?

The letter he had hoped for from Lord Henderson had not arrived. If it were true and Lord Henderson was not of this world any longer, was Sadie safe? He needed to know. Now that he was reconsidering his concerns in the light of day, it was time to go himself. Blast the post that never seemed to be reliable.

Later, when Richard was fresh from the stables and ready to get on with his latest business propositions, there was a knock on the door of the library. He had gained a reputation of being a shrewd businessman who could see a drowning business, decide he would either invest for a portion of the profits, or buy outright, make it sing again, and then resell it for a great profit.

She had been old enough to accept his intentions, but had she remained unattached? He wondered. The interest they shared when their eyes met was something he had never forgotten. Intelligent. Well-spoken. Maybe not a true beauty, as society would describe beauty, but she had been fresh and sweet, sassy and energetic. She would give him a merry chase. And there had been a growing love. Or he thought there had been until this most recent lack of response.

The footman entered and offered the post to Richard. He had expected some correspondence from several businessmen in a discussion of their respective properties. Richard turned his thoughts to the issues at hand. The first letter was an invitation he put to the side for his mother. There was a letter he had hoped would arrive soon, and there was another envelope written in a man's hand. Lord Henderson had penned it.

His groin tightened at the sudden reminder of his attraction to Sadie. Now it was likely too late, and this was information that she had been spoken for. He wasn't typically a person who thought of the worst outcomes, but things were different concerning Sadie. He had waited a year longer than he had intended and it would make sense if she had found another.

That was likely why he had not heard from her of late. It would have been highly improper for her to correspond with him if she were to marry another. However, it was equally improper for her or Lord Henderson not to inform him of her change of heart. He had made his intentions, if not formal, well known.

Where Sadie was now, he did not know. She wasn't Henderson's offspring for that good man and his wife had not been blessed with any, but they were very fond of her, so likely he would have provided for her. He would have given her a dowry or something upon marriage.

He had heard Horace Henderson's brother had a brood but, by all accounts, he was lazy. It seemed too bad that Horace and Lady Clarise had no children. They would have been superb parents, he imagined. But good for Sadie that they had been willing to be guardians of a kind.

Even if she didn't know anything about congress or the way to please a man, which it was likely she did not as Lady Clarise had died less than six months after that last meeting, he could teach her. He actually preferred to teach her, if he was given the opportunity. It was unfortunate that Horace had become something of a recluse once his wife became ill, and later, when she died, he was out only when necessary.

Henderson had sold all of his businesses because he had lost interest in them since losing Clarise. Some of which Richard had bought and had already turned into larger profit producers than they had been under Horace's hand. The land he had bought, he confided in Richard, was the income he had from tenants. He wanted Richard to take care of it for Sadie.

"Not your solicitor?" Richard had asked.

"Never trust your funds to anyone but your closest friends after you have gone on. They are not cared for properly. I trust you, Richard."

Richard sat in the library chair and opened up the missive with mixed hopes. The letter was dated December 15, 1811.

Richard,

I find myself more and more ill and the time has come that I finish the deed with Sarah. Please accept my agreement that if you are still interested in our Sarah, as I believe you were several months ago, she is yours to court and take to wife. Sarah does not know the content of this letter or even that I am penning it so keep it in case she needs proof of my permission.

She can be stubborn and hard to convince about things she has already set her mind to, but I am sure, with your loving direction, she will be able to learn to lean on your judgment when she needs it. I would like you to take on the property I have set up for you to maintain for Sarah. She is well trained on accounts but not much practical understanding as her livelihood never hinged on that knowledge.

It will not be an easy union at first. Society would not condone a man of your title and standing marrying a woman of no standing although we have always presented her as "lady", she is, in reality, the daughter of a servant. I assume you know that story but know she has been provided for if you choose not to continue your alliance.

Please be gentle with her. Show compassion for her losses. I don't believe you are anything like your sire or I would not agree to this union, but I know you to be honorable, protective, and upright, and you will take care of Sarah in the way that she has been taught is proper. In the way she deserves. She does not know of wifely ways with a husband so allow her to learn at your tender hand.

Lady Clarise and I have loved her wholly and if I should pass from this world into the next before you are married, then remember that I want you to take care of her for us. If it is not in marriage, then with that end in sight for her with an equal. Lord Jasper, maybe?

Until we meet again soon,

Horace Henderson, Viscount of Marston

Richard re-read the letter to make sure he understood the gist of the message. He meant for Richard to ask for Sadie's hand if Richard were still of the mind to do so. Suddenly his mood lightened. The thought of Jasper touching his Sadie caused great possessiveness to overtake him. She belonged to this duke, not that one.

Recalling what his mother had mentioned earlier in the week, *"Remember Richard, you are nearing thirty. Don't you agree it is time to find a woman that you can nurture into a duchess?"*

Richard laughed now as the women in his family had once again discussed his state of singleness. He took a sip of his tea as he remembered more of their conversation.

"Am I to understand that you are encouraging me to find a child bride?"

"Don't be ridiculous. Not a child, no. But a young woman not yet set in her ways may be a good choice."

"Possibly. Or a woman who knows what she wants and agrees it is life as my duchess."

And today as earlier in the week his mind called forth the mental picture of Sadie causing his trousers to tighten as his cock swelled with interest. Now that he knew she was to be his wife, he had much to do to prepare, starting with convincing her that this is the direction they both want to go. Show her that becoming his duchess was what she needed and desired.

The stay in London would be longer this year so that all would be settled before he brought her home to Amesbury House. His excitement was building. This would be more than an enjoyable trip to London this year; it would be life-changing.

Chapter 7 Time For a Daring Decision

Mr. Carraway, the family butler, brought in the mail and handed it to Richard who scanned the fronts and sat all down but the one from Lord Henderson. Upon opening it he saw the date was several months ago. He must have sent it right after Richard had left London on his last business trip. Odd that the response to his request for Sadie's hand arrived only yesterday and now this.

Since he had expected to do other things when he was in London before Julia and Mother arrived and the season began, he decided to get most of his business done early. Business like formally claiming Sadie's hand. He was eager to begin. Had the old gentleman changed his mind? Had Sadie?

It was unusual for a letter to take so long, never mind two, so it must have been diverted somehow. He sat in contemplation when Julia huffed in exasperation. When she had entered the room, he didn't know.

"Richard, the least you could do is give me the pink one. I know Mary has sent it to me."

Richard handed the envelope over with no other response. He opened the folded paper in his hand.

"Bloody hell," he exclaimed. "I was there not three months ago, and I could have settled this immediately while I was in London. I could have taken care of the entire issue. Evidently, the news we received this week is correct, and she is without protection. How must she have fared all alone?" The letter was sent by Mr. Shackleford, as written on the envelope. Lord Henderson had been dispatched to heaven and his dear wife, leaving Sadie to fend for herself.

Richard was walking around the room and talking when his sister inquired, "What is the matter, Richard? Who are you referring to?"

"I'm going ahead of you, Julia. You'll have to accompany mother with two extra footmen. I need to make sure the house is set up, the staff is ready for you, and to settle this urgent matter."

"Don't forget to deliver my letters when you get there."

"Leave any messages with my footman but do it today."

"But I still have one more to write. Richard, that is unkind of you."

"Then do it quickly, sister or it won't be delivered. I am leaving first thing in the morning."

"You were going to leave next week. What happened?"

He held up the paper in his hand. "This happened. I'm sorry, I'll share more when I can, but it must be addressed immediately."

His sister complained a little more, declaring he could at least reveal the reason, but one withering stare from him, quelled the discontent.

"Fine, brother, do what you must, but our Mother may have several items to send with you as well. Post being what it is these days, with many coaches ransacked and stolen from, I would prefer to know they got to their intended recipient."

That is what was likely the cause of the slow post. Richard made a mental note to add as many footmen as was feasible on his mother's journey to London. With any luck, both women would be settled in new homes within the year. He smiled even though he was trying to organize his thoughts.

Richard tried to interject a little humor. "Not worried your brother will be accosted on the road by bandits, then?"

"Of course not. Between your driver who looks like a bull, your tiger who takes his position to mean to be a tiger in the flesh, and your own presence, I have no fear for even the crown jewels to arrive safely," Julia said flippantly.

"Your confidence is appreciated and well-founded." He took a mock bow of acceptance. Julia laughed at her brother's lack of humility.

"When do you leave, dear?" asked Lady Margaret.

"Mother, I didn't see you come in. I plan to leave in the morning. How long before you follow?"

"I must wait for my companion to return from her visit with family, so at least two weeks. That allows us a few weeks to get our wardrobes in order before the first dinner parties begin. Julia needs a few more new gowns."

"And Mother should look for some as well if she is to be presentable. You might look for some new neckcloths."

"I assure you; I will look all the dash when escorting you, my dear sister."

Julia sniffed and feigned irritation. "See that you do, brother."

Richard was determined to find his little Darling and try to keep his friend's last request of him. Was Sadie in the same home or did that go with Henderson's estate? And if that were the case, it would make things harder. His mind went back to the young woman from the club. He knew he must have known her, it was only a matter of thinking harder. Would it matter now that he had a request from Henderson?

Possibly not, but until things were settled, there would be nothing he could do but go where life led him. His mind went to the woman he had passed outside of the group of solicitors' offices. He knew Henderson's attorney was Shackleford for it was also Jasper's representative. He had gone there that final week with Jasper to sign some papers before Jasper went abroad.

Then the same woman, he knew it was, ran into him when he was returning to leave business paperwork with his own solicitor, in the same building. She was familiar for a reason, he just didn't know what. And finally, the young woman looking over at the club those final days he was in London last, had to be so familiar because it must have been someone he had met in Henderson's home. Or near the time he had met Sadie or something similar. His Sadie was slenderer and less... endowed that the woman he had met. Dammit, why did it bother him so much? It made him realize that his Sadie may have been without support even before he left London and that stung. He would torment himself until he found her.

She didn't know where he was to send word of her need of him. He wasn't home. But even if he had been, there had not been any correspondence from her since Christmas. No, there was so much he didn't know and so much his princess had to answer for—as soon as he found her.

FINALLY IN LONDON, Richard was so eager to find his Duchess that he forgot his house would not be ready for several weeks, hence the need to stay in a room at the club. The first stop had been to see if he could get his townhouse a week early. It was good he didn't bring but his man, a maid, his driver and tiger. He could put them at Jasper's without any issues. The second had been to try and contact Sadie, only there was no answer at the door and the place looked empty. Damn. Now what was he do to? Where was he meant to look?

Jasper had not yet arrived from his trip on the continent because they had timed their arrivals to coincide. He loathed putting others out if he could find another way. So, other than placing his maid at Jaspers where she would be safe, there was no Henderson House, no rental ready as yet, no Jasper, so club it was. He and his three male employees would stay there.

What if Sarah did not agree to be with him? He didn't want to force her, but he already knew that they would suit. She may be unsure, but he'd take her home and then teach her to accept what they both knew they wanted. Their connection was immediate, and his cock grew just thinking about her.

If she ultimately refused, he would have to make sure she was introduced to others whom he knew to be nurturing and kind men. But he knew in his heart that it would not be necessary. Not sure he even could do that. He now was sure the woman he had seen that final week on several occasions was his princess.

No, he would not push but go slow. He was an organized man and the fact that his world was turned upside down drove him to rush and that was not how one conducted business. He was going to get a drink and calmly organize his thoughts and life. Formulate a full-proof plan and then execute it.

Richard leaned over to pour another finger of whiskey and slowly sipped the exceptional spirit. He rarely had more than one splash at a time, having been privy to what happened when he had too much. His time at University taught him more than academics. Seeing O'Leary at the door, he raised his hand in greeting. Fast on O'Leary's heels came Kendrick, then Ashton. After all were seated, Thayer entered the room.

Thayer nodded to the rest. "What have we here? All but Jasper and Trenton today. Are we all that parched or that desperate to leave our wives to their own devices for a spell?" he laughed. O'Leary laughed. "I'm always parched. I expected the others were as well, but did'na expect you, Amesbury."

"I arrived a few weeks early. There is a reason."

"Ah, yes, the lovely young lady you haven't been able to forget. I thought you were enamored with the young girl at Henderson's," said O'Leary.

"Have you not heard?" asked Kendrick. "He has gone on. I heard most of his possessions went to his brother, but as his brother would not come into London, not even to bury his only sibling, he had a few things sent to him and sold the rest."

Ashton shook his head in disbelief. "What a fool. I understand not liking London. It can be a damned dirty place. But to leave your brother's things just to the auction block? Unheard of."

"And what about the young girl, Amesbury? Do you know?" Thayer inquired. "I believe you had hoped for an understanding before tragedy hit both families. My condolences, by the way."

The others added their sympathies as well.

"There have been several developments since I was last here. In the last week, actually. I had sent a letter requesting to declare for Sadie... Sarah, the woman under Henderson's care. I had not heard back at all. I now find that the timing was unfortunate for he was not well, even then.

"He had sent a response that, as the fates would allow, did not arrive until yesterday week. Then, on the morning I was to come here to remedy the issue with Sarah, I received another letter from Henderson, posthumously, through the solicitor. I was just at the Henderson House home a day ago, and... that's it! Bloody hell!" Richard lowered his voice.

The Laird gave Richard an odd look. "What are you on about, man?"

"I knew I had met that girl before. The one I ran into outside the solicitor's office during my last trip. It was her, Sarah. She was considerably more physically matured, and even her voice was more refined, sad. I didn't recognize her blossoming body and her sad tone. Sarah was so lively and sent barbs my way and waited for my response. This was a different woman I met."

He shook his head in disbelief. "Henderson must have passed the same week I left London, and I didn't know. I could have made life so much easier for her. The girl on the corner. Also, her. They looked the same, in the same coat. Do you think she was trying to find one of us?"

"You," said Trenton. "If she was looking for any one of us, it would have been you. But why? How would she know you would have been here?"

"Several of you met her at Henderson's that evening before we left. You may not remember as you were either newly married, muddled with romantic thoughts, or seeking another. What a fool I have been not to recognize her straightaway."

Richard felt the churning of anticipation and irritation in his gut. She would have known him immediately. Was she so grief-stricken that she had no awareness of her surroundings? Possibly, but she would answer to him for stationing herself on the Corner of Indiscretion. Where else had she gone? What had she subjected herself to after her protector had passed away?

Ashton shook his head in disbelief. "Okay, let me get this straight. First, in January, after another year of not seeing Sarah, but I assume you were corresponding, you passed a woman that seemed familiar, but she did not recognize you either. Then the girl on the corner that reminded you of Sarah, you now believe might have been her. Then, you go home and send a letter asking to court Sarah. No return response was received until a week ago, directly after you learn of Henderson's death. After that, just as you were coming to consummate the arrangement, you received a letter from the solicitor, but written in Henderson's hand, reiterating the same as the first letter and verifying his death."

"Yes, that sounds right."

"And now," added Trenton, "you want to find Sarah but cannot so far."

"Yes."

Kendrick shook his head. "The woman on the corner was shrouded in a voluminous coat and ample hood, if I remember correctly. You could not have known it was her. I'm rather impressed you felt she was familiar to you."

"Well, at least you now have a place to find her current details," said O'Leary. "If nothing else, it will ease your mind. You'll have the address and anything else he is privy to if you add some coin to his pocket."

"Not this solicitor. That is why Jasper and Henderson liked him. I doubt he would share something like that. It would make his client vulnerable, and some of these men have morals."

"I much prefer doing business in Scotland. They aren't the kind to keep a man from his lass." The Scotsman shook his head.

"I had thought to go to the townhouse, but it looked as though no one was home when I was on my way to the rented Dwyer House earlier. It has been several months since his passing. I suppose the solicitor is the only next solution."

Thayer leaned back in his cushioned armchair and twirled the amber liquid in the crystal glass. "Have you tried knocking on the townhouse door? Just because it appears quiet doesn't mean it is empty. Would she have any house help? Maybe not. She might be waiting on you to return."

"It's been three months. Why would you think that she would still be there?" Ashton took a sip of his drink.

"Well, if Henderson favored her, and she was left destitute after he died, I believe he would have made some kind of provision for Sarah."

Richard answered Ashton. "He did. He lived in London, not just rented for a season. Living in his home would have made it easy, but if he didn't tell you in his letter where to find her, then he would likely have left her set up where you could find her."

Kendrick nodded as he sat his empty glass down on the center table. "That's right. And he adored that girl. He had given the estate to his brother to live in, but the income had to be divided between them. He had investments separate from the estate."

Richard nodded. "So, it would follow that he owned his home. I've rented just down from Henderson House. I'll make a stop there this evening when I should be able to see any light."

"That's settled then. Tell me your plans while you are here," Ashton said. "Are we to have a wedding?"

"That is my plan. And my sister Julia is becoming fully engaged in the season's events this year, having been robbed of it last year due to the duke's passing."

"Yes, I hope your mother has fared well."

"She has, thank you. Thayer, you'll enjoy this tidbit. Mother has decided to throw her lace handkerchief in the circle as well this year."

"Indeed. Good for her. Only grown children now, and if Julia makes a good match this season, there won't be any reason to stay home. How do you feel about that?"

The men kept up a great round of conversation, moving through each household as though they hadn't spoken only a few months before. Finally, they rose to leave, each offering to entertain him at their homes. Richard declined but agreed to meet up the next midday.

"I'll have a quick run by Henderson's and if I don't find her, I'll be back here to outline my strategy."

Grabbing a hack, he drove by the Henderson House and saw minimal candlelight, but it was enough to tell him there were people in residence. He knocked again. No one there. Or rather, no one was answering. He didn't want to make a scene, but he did call out to her and tried the door. Deciding she wasn't there, Richard turned to leave. The door opened by a less than formal, rather young gentleman Richard had never seen before.

"Good evening."

Richard noticed the lack of "Sir" and thought it odd. "Yes, I'm here for a moment of Sarah's time. It is important."

"I'm sorry but there are no inhabitants. I am keeping the place secure. Nothing more. Good night."

Richard didn't pry further but continued on to see what his townhouse was looking like now that its owner had also died. There was something peculiar about the man who answered. Would a watchman answer the door at all? Or would you forget to add sir to every response? And would you be so young? Richard doubted it. After checking the rental property that should be ready soon, he finished back at the club. After dinner, he chatted with acquaintances and then went for an early night.

He had a significant task in front of him tomorrow. His house would be ready in the morning and his London staff was at the ready to do the final set up today and tomorrow. He would stay there tomorrow. He intended to find his girl and begin the wooing. Once he had her tethered to him, Richard would discuss her presence on the Corner of Indiscretion and the exact penalty for her unfortunate and dangerous choices.

If she had known he was the man she passed at the solicitors, why the hell had she not said something to him? She was left with no protection, no benefactor. She had a lot to explain, that was for sure.

Chapter 8 Time For The Hunt

F rustration oozed from Richard. He had not expected to have such difficulty finding Sarah, but without a surname, her common given name was making finding her almost impossible. She had always been referred to as Lady Sarah and in most cases, that was all he had ever heard anyone call her except when he called her Sadie.

What was Lord Henderson about sending him such a cryptic and yet directive letter? Could the man have not spoken to him in the beginning? Used plain language? If one knew the Daring Duke at all well, they would not have even questioned his tenacity in finding the object of his desire. But being that man was often a maddening thing. This would consume him to it's end.

Once he settled on a business to buy and restore, envisioned a piece of property to resell, or made some other decision for changes on his estate, he didn't listen to naysayers. Popular opinion never meant much to him as he grew into his future title. Because he was so often right and never disastrously wrong, most simply stood by to see what he had in mind.

When Richard had decided that Sarah was the one for him, when the young woman had not been completely shocked at his forwardness, he found he had become obsessed with her. Since that moment and the conversation with his friends, he had spent the last two evenings devising his next move. He wasn't above knocking on select doors in search of her. Possibly hiring Bow Street Runners if necessary. Yes, that was an excellent idea.

What a damn fool he'd been not to inquire when Henderson was alive what her surname was. She had never disclosed on the envelopes or letterhead for they were always entitled, Henderson House. Even her seal was an "S" for Sarah or Sadie.

The estate that Henderson had released to his brother some years ago was in the north of England and it was useless to send a message to inquire with him.

Horace Henderson had been quite clear that his brother, while decent enough, had only enough thought in his head to keep the estate with guidance from Horace from afar. Leaving to visit his brother in London or taking interest in anything else, was more than he was capable of, so Richard considered that a dead end. Sarah would not have gone there.

What was even more ire-raising was this morning, when he had finally seen some signs of life in the daylight and had knocked on the door of the late Lord Henderson. The inhabitants would surely know something. Maybe some of the staff had stayed behind and the young man who answered had been visiting them or more likely, just a young servant for they wouldn't need a butler with no person in residence.

At first, he had thought there was no one at home, because there was no immediate answer. Which would be odd since there were signs that someone must be in residence. Finally, the door had been opened to him and a rather odd, older character that the last time, stood before him. As though he were performing a part that he was unfamiliar with.

"Good morning to you. I am here to call on Lady Sarah." He had nothing else to call her, so he tried not to stumble at the lack of surname.

"You are mistaken, sir."

"Am I?"

"These are not visiting hours." There was a pause. "Sir."

Hmm, the sir was an afterthought that spoke of a person not long in service and no little disrespect. But there was no invitation to return during the appropriate time nor to leave his calling card. Both were suspicious.

Richard smiled through his unease with the man before him. "Quite right, but Sarah and I have a special relationship. She is my intended and I will see her."

"Unfortunately, there is no Sarah here." Which was off because he'd all but admitted she was there by stating it wasn't visiting hours.

"You and I both know that is not true. I will leave my card."

"For whom, sir?"

Frustrated, Richard replied. "The lady of the house, Sarah. I will return during visiting hours, and you will let me in."

He held out his card for several long moments before the butler took the card offering Richard his opportunity to step into the entranceway.

He called out "Sarah," but there was no reply. He tried, "Sadie." with the same result. Fearing he was in the wrong and cursing that he did not have her last name, he called out "Princess," knowing that if she were in residence, his Sadie would storm out and demand he stop using that endearment. Nothing.

Finally, with no way to back up his accusations, he stormed out of the front door and slammed it behind him. He rarely opened or closed his own doors, but his anger was so intense and his fear that something was terribly wrong that he deviated from his typical behavior. He would find her if he had to take this place apart bit by bit, but first, he needed to gain some vital information and create a plan. And gather reinforcements.

Rarely had the duke wanted to use his name, title, and clout to force an outcome, but this was most definitely one of them. He still wondered if he should gather his friends and make that a reality. Why his gut told him something was wrong, he didn't know, but it was such a fierce knowledge, his mind, and body protested when he walked away. He would not walk away again.

For the rest of the morning, Richard worried about the encounter at Henderson House. It was time to set off for the solicitor's offices. He and Henderson had made use of the same solicitor at one time but when Jasper took on the man for his own representation, Richard found another in the same offices. And while he might have strong thoughts on the matter of privacy, he hoped he could impress upon the man that he was indeed looking out for the young lady's best interests.

After all, it was the solicitor who sent the letter, if the words on the page were to be believed. Henderson wasn't a cryptic man usually, but when it came to Sarah, he had been closed-mouthed and would start to share things about her and then stop. He remembered one incident in particular.

"She will need a diligent husband when she is ready. That girl is strong-minded and determined when she sees a prize and desires it. Much like you, I would imagine."

"Is that a good quality in a wife?" Richard had asked.

"Doesn't matter for she is not ready to marry."

And the conversation was stopped and redirected but it left Richard wondering why he would have brought up the subject at all. He hated all the damn secrecy then and now.

Two hours later, he emerged from the offices of Shackleford and Shackleford frustrated, but with at least one victory. He knew her surname, Morgan. Her name was quite common but being a Scotch Irish name, possibly she had relatives in Ireland or Scotland for he knew there were none nearby. He'd inquire of O'Leary. Not that the man knew the whole of his country but there was a possibility she had been there since Henderson hailed from the north of England.

He'd wanted more information, but Shackleford refused more than the cryptic response of, "You'll know where to go to find her, if you think on it."

His obsession was growing. Likely not a healthy thing but determination was how he made a good living for his estate and family, and it was what would see him through to the end to find his soon-to-be wife. Thankfully, his sister and mother were yet to arrive, giving him more freedom of movement without prying family members.

Richard looked up to see Jasper's long stride bringing his friend closer. Good. He was back and would be in for a good hunt. Pouring him a drink, Richard settled in to listen to Jasper's news of the continent before speaking.

"Something felt off," finished Richard. "I want to go back."

Jasper took another sip of his fine whiskey and sat back.

"Tell me why. I mean, it really could be the wrong lady of the house. Henderson House must surely have been sold."

"I don't know how to explain it, but I honestly believe that something is wrong. The watchman who answered was not respectful. Then the butler was not right. He wasn't as confident as the butler Lord Henderson employed. This one appeared to be uncomfortable, like he was hiding something and feared discovery."

Richard stopped his brain from going to the long end of the stick as to just what could be wrong. It took a great deal of effort on his part to not push harder immediately and force his friend to go with him to confront the unknown danger. Instead, he tried to focus on the more likely situation. It was too early for her to be out, normally, therefore it was more likely that she no longer lived here. But the man left him with a feeling of wrongness. Richard had made several fortunes by listening to his inner voice.

Finally, after having a light morning meal, Richard persuaded Jasper to go with him to the house.

"If, after we have tried to gain access to Lady Sarah you are convinced that I am wrong, then I will search elsewhere."

"I'm always up for an adventure. But here is Lord Thayer and company. I believe they are intent on inviting you to dinner tonight at O'Leary's house. Accept, my friend. They are a pleasant diversion of which you are in great need."

Richard ignored Jasper openly but inwardly wondered if he was right. Had he become too focused on someone who might not even accept him with his different needs? How did he reveal those needs without scaring her off? He stood and shook hands with Trenton who led the others as they entered the establishment at their leisure. He was the latest to marry and the least likely to come around, so he counted it as good fortune that he was among the group.

Ashton spoke first. "We've been to the docks to check on the things there. Jasper had been to the Continent, and Trenton? Well, we know what he has been occupied with. But what of you, my Lord Griffin?"

"I believe the address is Your Grace, now," said Jasper.

The others murmured responses. "Yes, but if any of you should refer to me as that in private, I shall have your head."

O'Leary smiled. "Not quite in your power, I'm thankful to say."

Trenton followed Richard's glance out the window with a view to the corner intersection. "He sells wares."

"Wares?" asked O'Leary.

Trenton nodded as he accepted a crystal glass with a bit of whiskey. "The man on the corner. His wares are mostly women. My Sofia says the women are down on their luck."

O'Leary frowned. "Surely all the women that man comes in contact with are not women with ulterior motives."

His friend nodded. "Possibly. But if they aren't already in the man's clutches, and haven't already warmed a few beds, that situation will surely end soon."

"I should have gone out there and inquired to see if it was my Sarah when I saw her out there on my last trip. I won't ever forgive myself if it was her. I fear it was."

"I still don't quite understand why you would even think she was that woman. She would have had servants to do her bidding soon after his death. I am positive that Henderson would not have left her penniless." Trenton took another sip.

"He didn't, if his final solicitor's letter was any indication," said Richard. "But Trenton, I must ask, how is it that your duchess knows of these unsavory realities?"

"It is a long story, but if you get your Darling Duchess, I am sure you will become as well educated as we have become, of the social ills of England."

As though Kendrick understood his dilemma and the associated fear, he leaned closer to Richard and spoke into his ear.

"If it is your Sarah, I am sure she would not have been there for what it is known for, even if it's a well-established corner. Henderson did not leave her destitute nor would he have left her uneducated as to how to live after he was gone." Richard nodded. Kendrick was right.

His Sarah. Was he going mad? No, he remembered his friends when they were trying to win the hand of their beloveds. Crazy was the reality until they married. Richard realized that over the years he assumed she would be his or at least open to the exploration and that, therefore, made her his. An error, possibly, but that was how Lord Henderson had encouraged him to think. That it was a possibility regardless of his station in life and hers.

"Well then," declared Thayer, "if the young woman was there for no other reason but to be curious or defiant, she deserves a switching and if I were her father, be it Sarah or another, I would be more than happy to accommodate and educate on that little indiscretion."

"Or her papa," said Trenton.

"Indeed," said Ashton.

Ashton had said very little as though he were thinking of another time. All these men had wives who were, indiscreet on occasion, and had made some colossal poor decisions. Their Little ladies were well acquainted with the flat of their husbands' hands.

Richard looked at Thayer and then the Scot beside him. O'Leary, an outspoken man who wasn't often in London but came when his wife missed her dear friend, Lady Ashton. Now, he understood the women were all great friends. He'd like his wife to become part of that lot. O'Leary laughed and slapped Richard on the back.

"Well, the lass is lucky if she makes it home to her father. I fear she stood on the corner just a wee bit too long not to be of some understanding of the goings on there."

Thayer shook his head in disagreement. "I don't think so. The man makes his money by gaining the confidence of the young girls by protecting them at first. Buying them trinkets, helping them to dress a little better to attract a specific clientele. When they need a place to sleep later that evening, he offers a place for them. If you're on the street sometimes it's all you can do. The young lady in question seemed well-dressed and well cared for."

Jasper asked, "How do you know so much about it?"

Ashton sighed and answered for them all. "Wives. Like Trenton said, when you acquire a wife, you also acquire a long list of charities that they speak passionately about. As their husbands, we are encouraged to listen."

O'Leary laughed boisterously which drew the hard stares of several gentlemen in the room. "And throw coin at them. The wives and the charities."

Kendrick laughed. "Lady Ashton is especially energetic in her charity work."

"So, you think that's what is going on with anyone there?" asked Richard.

Lord Thayer shrugged. "I do not know. She was likely one to attempt to entice the women off the street employment rather than join them. Shall we go ask?"

Lord Ashton sighed. "Better we watch what's going on over there and not interrupt unless there is a need. Griffin's lady isn't there right now, anyway. In fact, I haven't noticed her for months."

Trenton nodded. "Understood. The group of us will take care of putting extra eyes on the situation and if any of us should feel there is cause to intervene, we won't hesitate to do so."

"I know it sounds incredibly stupid. What concern is her situation to me? Especially with the concerns over Sarah, but I feel they may be connected."

"You have amazing insight into situations of business. I can't but believe you have no less into human nature," pointed out Jasper.

Kendrick nodded. "I think most of us know exactly how you feel. And, if you think it is important to intervene, we shall be there beside you, taking care of the problem.

O'Leary bounced forward and grabbed his crystal cut-glass of fine whiskey. "That settled, do you need us to find your little lady?"

"Darling," corrected Ashton.

Richard nodded. "Precisely so."

The group of men nodded sagely. Kendrick added, "And that makes the entire ordeal difficult as hell."

It was quiet as the men sat silently contemplating their glasses of whiskey.

"I have the solicitor's follow-up letter."

"Do you?" asked Kendrick.

Richard nodded and produced the missive from inside his waistcoat. Thayer reached out his hand. "May I?"

Griffin,

I am dying. I feel my body give up the fight but while I still can, I want to settle things between us. Sarah needs a husband and we have not procured one for her as I was loathe to give her up. She has been such a companion to Clarise and I, but it was selfish.

She is old enough to wed and I should have set my mind to accomplish that task before I left this earth. I now rely on you to do so. She is now a woman of means if she followed my direction and is therefore, in need of a guardian.

I give you the task but would desire that alliance to be much more than that of caretaker and ward. I would want her to find a husband and would be delighted if you were agreeable that it be you. At any turn, she is yours to take care of if you will.

She is where you would expect, likely lost in the world without a caretaker, and feeling desperate for someone to help her navigate the world. We have taught her much, and she is a stubborn one, but also clever, inventive, and capable of great love. Go to her and do what you can. I know you once desired her; may I dare ask that you love her?

Yours with confidence and affection,

Lord Horace Henderson

Viscount of Marston

Lord Thayer asked quietly, "Have you thought about how that's going to happen even if you find her?"

Richard sighed. "The convincing? It's not something that I can go up to a young prospect and say, *May I spank your arse when you are naughty and then cuddle you?*"

The Laird O'Leary chuckled quietly. "*Or may I spank you when we are intimate, and you please me?*"

Richard shook his head. "*Nor can I say, Sarah, this is how it will be, because she will reject me out of hand.*"

"I found that with Annalise, I knew she was my Little lady. So, I simply married her. The rest sorted itself out without too much fanfare. Women are emotional creatures. Deciding quickly prevents that early angst that can give way to denying you both what you want simply out of fear or uncertainty."

"I have spanked her for her sharp tongue and rudeness, but I didn't do more than cuddle and be affectionate afterward. She needs more understanding of the situation than that."

"Not always," said Thayer.

"I don't miss those days of indecision." Ashton leaned back contemplatively.

Jasper nodded at Richard, and he leaned in to tell the group of his recent experience in trying to contact Henderson's Sarah.

Richard pointed out something in the letter. "Henderson said she is where I would expect her to be. What the hell does that mean exactly? It isn't exactly a map. Where do I go next?"

"Actually, it is," said Thayer. "Look there is a comma after that first clause, making the next one a completely different statement."

Jasper continued. "So where do you expect to find her?"

"At Henderson House?" asked Richard.

"Worth another try then," said Jasper. "You were on the right track."

"Anyway, first find Sarah, then my intentions are to address the issue of a wife. And I shall rely on you and your beautiful ladies to help me put her at ease."

"Could Sarah be the one? Really your Little Darling?" asked Ashton.

"It appears that Henderson may have thought so," answered Thayer.

"So do I or I would not be here doing this." Richard spoke with new authority.

"Indeed," said Kendrick.

Jasper turned to look at the newest leg-shackled man of their group. "Trenton, it's good to see you out today. But I had thought your new bride would have kept you away this season."

"Yes, she has rather kept me busy, but she wouldn't be away from the season for any longer than she needed to. She is a Londoner you know and being in the country is something that takes a little time to get used to. Not to mention that she has plenty of encouragement to not let the season pass without her experiencing it." Trent shrugged nonchalantly. "Besides, she's less well-behaved in London, which gives me more opportunities to enjoy the side effects of her little indiscretions."

The men chuckled and nodded in agreement. After informing the gentlemen where he and Jasper had intended to go, he agreed that he would come to dinner and meet them to update them on the happenings.

Thayer nodded. "Annalise would be delighted if you found and brought Miss... Lady..."

"Morgan."

"Miss Morgan... with you. Is she Lady Morgan?"

"I don't believe so. She was called Lady Sarah because of her association with the viscount. Her mother, his previous housekeeper, passed away when Sarah was eleven. I have decided upon lady. She is not likely to notice one way or the other and soon she should be a duchess."

"The ladies will be glad to add her to their company, at any rate. But don't be so sure about women and what they notice. It is quite disturbing sometimes."

"Thank you, Thayer. I shall remember that. Until dinner, then."

Chapter 9 Time For Ingenuity

They were there when she arrived back from the market and visiting with the Arnolds. Without a key, the very people she had sent away via Mr. Arnold had entered her home, uninvited not one week later. Sarah had been very careful to keep things locked but it was no deterrent to these people. Mrs. Flander was a very angry woman and had dismissed her maid without so much as a by your leave. She also turned away every applicant sent over until no more showed.

Unfortunately, there was no way that Sarah could slip out. She tried and tried for over a week, but they seemed to know where she was at all times, and when she did get out, they would appear out of nowhere and usher her back home in hurried steps.

She told them her solicitor paid all her bills, and she did not have a need for money, which seemed to anger them even more.

"Then we will use your accounts for the things we want."

Mrs. Flander tried to go to the dressmakers, because no woman that had ever lived in the house had such a girth as Mrs. Flander and there were no clothing at the ready anywhere. That meant she needed new clothing. She attempted to go to the dressmakers and commission a few dresses, however, the modiste turned her away.

"She said if I didn't bring my mistress with me, then she needed the money upfront. When I used your name, she declined to serve me because she said the order always came through Lord or Lady Henderson."

They were becoming angry that they couldn't seem to find any money and the solicitor had sewn up the accounts, requiring Sadie to come in and assure them that it was okay to continue services. She refused, but she was becoming more frightened of what they would do next.

The older boy, whom they called Pick, and Mrs. Flander, were the ones that were the scariest. Pick had struck her in the face when she wouldn't go to the solicitor's office with him to get the money. She said it was the arrangement set by Lord Henderson, and she had nothing to do with it, nor could she change it. Mrs. Flander told him he could not mar her or cause her any physical harm, for she was the only face that seemed to use the accounts.

"As it is, that mark might take too long to lighten enough to no longer be noticeable to do what we need done."

Then, last night, they had hidden her away when Richard had arrived. Then earlier today, when Richard came to the door, she was hidden away again. To the cellar. When she would make noise, he didn't hear her. She heard him call out for her but soon it was silent again. Sarah was heartbroken when he went away without persevering.

"Is this man that is demanding to see you, your betrothed?"

Sarah didn't hesitate. "Yes. He has been gone to his estate to take care of business and his family. I expected him at any time."

"And you said nothing." Mrs. Flander seemed flustered.

"I didn't think I needed to, and then I didn't want to."

Pick raised his hand again to Sarah, but Mrs. Flander pushed him away. "You are going to ruin it all. We must think about what we are to do."

However, the Flanders people, for she knew they were not all kin, now, must have decided that after peering in the windows, then driving by knocking not once but twice and demanding entrance the second time, he was trouble. Then, when he appeared this morning demanding to be allowed entrance, the Flanders became restless.

With the certainty that Richard would not stop coming to the house until he had spoken to Sarah, Mrs. Flander decided it was time to get rid of her. Pick knew just where they could take her.

"There is a man who claimed to own Carrington Corner. It's a perfect place to dispose of problems."

Sadie knew exactly where that corner was. She had stayed far enough away from that man when she previously went there to draw the attention of Richard or some of the young lords that had frequented Lord Henderson's home. She had hoped she could make contact right after Lord Henderson died but it was winter and likely not anyone was out and about. No one came to retrieve her from the street.

Finally, when she knew Richard was gone, she couldn't return because it was becoming too dangerous. The man tried to say she owed him for standing on his block and especially his corner. This was the same place that Mrs. Arnold had brought her to point out the club that she knew Lord Henderson and the men who visited him, used.

The little troublesome man sent her away. "I conduct business here. If you aren't part of my business, then you must go, milady."

She did have business, but not with him. She would have pounded on the club door if she had thought it wouldn't have ruined her new reputation as a woman of leisure.

It didn't take them long to figure things out and soon the eldest son had somehow hired a hackney, held a knife to her side, and demanded she get in the coach. When the coachman offered to help the lady, he had been rebuffed. Pick told the man something, and the carriage lurched into movement.

"Where are we going?" Sadie demanded. She knew but she wanted verification.

"You'll find out. I wonder how much money you are worth?" The sneer in his voice curdled her stomach.

"What?" Sarah hadn't thought he would sell her. Dear God.

"I know a man who pays well for women. They don't last long with him, but once he finds a good buyer, he doesn't keep you anyway. More profitable for him to use before selling slightly used merchandise unless it is pristine. Are you pristine, madam?"

She had heard of men selling their daughters but that couldn't be what he was talking about. No, that corner and that man now made sense. She had to do something. Sadie rocked the carriage. He pressed the knife to her waist again putting just enough pressure to stop her movements.

"You know, I like the feel of a blade going through flesh. It's satisfying. I'm to deliver you with no more blemishes than your bruised cheek, but I have been known to lose control when I am angry. You don't want to see that, Lady Morgan. It isn't very pretty."

Sarah would agree that it wouldn't be very attractive at all. Why had she not sent that letter to Richard when she discovered she had a house and no servants? Or even when she had discovered her mistake in hiring the Flanders. That is what the Arnolds had told her to do. Now all she wanted was Richard, no matter how displeased he would be with her, she would be safe.

Tears silently slid down her cheeks as she remembered Richard was so close. He had admonished her to contact him or those who resided in London if she needed anything. Her protector was trying to see her and find her but was denied entrance. Now, if he were to walk the whole of the house, he wouldn't find her for she would not be there.

Tears for the lost opportunity with Lord Griffin and her lack of truth-telling when the Arnolds asked what she would do when Lord Henderson passed. They would have stayed, had they known. She would have paid them well. Her life would have been so much different. Happy.

And if she had behaved better, maybe Richard would have taken her before Lord Henderson had passed away. Then she would have never had to deal with the mess her life was now. She needed a papa to take care of her. No, she'd never had a papa but a protector, yes. She needed Richard in whatever form he took.

The hack rolled up to a small house right across from the club and next to the corner where she had stood when trying to find her lord who would be a duke. He was a duke now. Would he still frequent the club? Might any of his acquaintances be there now? Might he?

When the carriage stopped, the man with greasy hair and sour-smelling clothing came out of the little house. Sarah was forced out onto the roadside by knifepoint. She stumbled and screamed, but the knife dug into her hip painfully, silencing any further distressed sounds from her. She felt warmth seep into her undergarment.

Her tears fell fast and furious but Pick and the little, disgusting man seemed to not notice or care. Pick held her arm with one hand and pressed the knife firmly into her side while they spoke. Sarah decided that she would have to figure something out or she would be sold to the man whose manner, appearance, and smell made her want to retch. She did gag once, and the men laughed.

"You'll soon stop that my girl," said the revolting man.

She sent a pleading look in the direction of the gentlemen's club and the repulsive man laughed again.

"Those men are no gentlemen, milady. They are men who do unmentionable things to their women. You do not want to entice one of them to your bed."

He put his hand to his chin. "Or maybe you do. I can get more for a woman like that. What do you say?"

"If you can get more for her then you will pay more for her," said Pick.

When the man reached into his pocket and pulled out a small bag of coin, Sadie had a fleeting thought that it was now or never. Pick moved the knife and let go of her arm to grab the money and when he did, Sarah grabbed her skirts, pushed the bag from the man's hand, and ran for all she was worth.

As a child, she would outrun the other children and even older ones. She liked winning and practiced whenever she could but that had been a long time ago. Now it would come in handy if she could get her body to remember. She set the next street as her goal and once there she would go wherever there were people.

JASPER AND RICHARD arrived at the door of Henderson House and found the odious man still attending the entrance. Unfortunately for him, Richard was not prepared to repeat the morning's interactions.

"Before you say anything, sir, I must inform you that Lady Sarah has declined permission to meet with you."

"She has, has she? I prefer to hear that from her, and not a servant at the door. And You are speaking to the Duke of Amesbury."

Richard allowed his voice to take on a haughty tone, and he made sure his body language echoed that tone. He watched as the man before him hesitated and even took one step back as though the Duke of Amesbury, might be more than he could handle.

"I am sorry my lord, but it is not going to happen today."

"My lord? Did you not hear my title? Duke. You will address me accordingly."

The man hesitated. "Your Grace, you cannot see her today."

"Ah," said Richard, "so she will see me tomorrow. And if I wish not to wait until tomorrow and demand to see her today, what will you do?"

Jasper spoke to Richard in serious tones that Richard understood as a pretense for the servant's benefit, hoping to get a better response. "Now Your

Grace, we don't want to trouble the man if he's following Lady Sarah's instructions."

The butler hesitated and then replied. "Thank you, sir."

"However," continued Jasper, "if she has not instructed him to turn you away at the door, or you feel there is some subterfuge in his communication, I don't see how we could let that go unaddressed. And we would at least have to inform your solicitor and Mr. Shackleford."

"Shackleford? Sir, I assure you that these are Lady Sarah's instructions."

Richard barged past the butler while saying, "I don't believe you."

Jasper followed behind Richard and the flustered man stumbled with sounds of surprise, but no words would form. As Richard looked around the foyer, he stalked down the receiving hall into the first room. Jasper stayed on his heel and the butler followed sputtering.

"Sir."

The men continued to walk further into the house.

"My lord."

Neither gentleman slowed their forward motion.

"Your Grace."

Richard stopped and turned at the last address.

"Where is she?"

"You are trespassing, Your Grace."

"Am I?" Richard had taken on the intense, lord-in-charge mannerism that had allowed him to bluff through even the toughest business transaction. "Only if Lady Sarah has denied me, and she has not. Not only is she to be my wife, she is my ward. Soon this will be my home, so heed me well. Better you bring her to me or bring me to her and we will settle this now. Then you can go about your duties, and I won't make sure you're thrown into Newgate."

"She is not here," hissed the doorman with only a slight bit of deference.

"Shouldn't that be, she is not in residence? No, you are no butler. Who are you?"

Richard wondered who this man was and what was going on. The violence he felt toward the staff member gave him pause to think he was emotionally invested in this outcome and that he could easily lose control. But he was invested. It was Sarah and she was his.

Suddenly, he now believed that there was more than Sarah hesitating to see him after such a long absence between them. Something sinister may be at hand and that frightened him and angered him more than he could ever imagine. And damn but he still didn't know if it had anything to do with *his* Sarah or another.

"Who isn't here? Be specific." Richard demanded.

"Lady Sarah is out."

"But you said I was mistaken. No Sarah was here, then unavailable, and now not here. Maybe I am in error and the only way to prove it one way or the other is to show me. After all, Sarah is a rather common name."

"Which Sarah were you inquiring after?" asked the obviously overwhelmed man.

"How many Sarahs do you have in residence? What is your Lady Sarah's last name and who else is in this house?" asked Jasper to keep the man off guard.

"Wouldn't you know, milord? Your Grace?"

Richard was through. He was getting inside every room of this house to see for himself and stalking through the house, if need be, to make sure it wasn't Sarah Morgan amongst the persons here. If they had hurt one hair on her head, by God...

"As I have stated. I am the Duke of Amesbury, and Sarah is my betrothed. She has lived here her whole life from the day she was born until now. I will bring in the constable if you cannot prove to me who lives here."

That did it. The man's eyes widened in fearful surprise. Slowly he regained control of his features, and his face went bland again, but this time it took great effort to do so.

"Then she will know where to find you, I imagine, sir."

"Which tells me you do not know her, or you would have been informed. I have not seen you before. Where is Mr. Arnold?" Richard asked as he strode deeper into what he remembered to be a receiving room.

He stayed his immediate habit of removing his gloves and hat and instead turned back to fix a demanding stare on the man in front of him. Both seemed to have forgotten poor Jasper who was examining items in the rooms. The doorman was nonplussed. He scoured the next room, the library, and saw some of Sarah's comfort items. She had a soft doll and several soft animal toys, all well-made with fine hand stitching. He reached down and snatched up the rabbit made of a real rabbit pelt that he had brought her the second time he had come to visit her. He shoved the soft toy into his pocket.

"Your Grace, that belongs to one of the children."

"No, it does not. It belongs to Sarah. I gave it to her."

Richard called her name and when he had no response, went upstairs in search of her wardrobe. He was certain the room was hers by the disarray, and the gown he had seen her wear on one occasion was found lying on the bed.

Richard had memorized the shoes she wore inside, soft kitten slippers that were often pink, a favorite color of hers. The clothing she had worn each time he came to visit with Lord Henderson, in the closet amongst many he had never seen. There, in the back of the first wardrobe was the gown she wore when he had taken four turns about the parlor because it was the right number for a visit, she had informed him. His heart hurt and his stomach seized in fear.

"Sir, I must ask you to leave," said the stupid man.

"Jasper, this is Sarah's clothing." Richard reached back in the wardrobe and pulled out the black woolen long coat with a hood. "I knew that was her. She was within my grasp, and I didn't know it."

Jasper turned to his friend. "Your Grace, are you sure this is hers?"

"Yes, and these, her slippers. She is here, by God and I mean to find her."

The butler or doorman or whatever he was, seemed to not know what to say. The fear was clearly written on his face and Richard wondered if he was trying to find a way to escape. A buxomly woman rounded the corner.

"What is the ruckus? I thought when we had shut that girl up, there would be no more trouble."

"Mrs. Flander," began the man who stood trembling before the enraged lord and his companion.

"Don't Mrs. Flander me, man. I have rooms to lighten of their valuables and... oh! Who are you?" The woman seemed to get her wits about her and demanded, "What are you doing in my house?"

"Your house? Lady Sarah's house, I believe you mean."

If he weren't so angry and now frightened for his lady, he would have appreciated the woman's ability to think on her feet. Right now, it simply infuriated him further.

"Of course, milord."

"Your Grace, if you don't mind."

The woman took a solid breath as though to calm herself. "I'll go and fetch her, milord, Your Grace."

Richard took a step closer to the doorway and the woman. "No, I'll come with you. Jasper, stay with this man."

"But she is dressing, Your Grace." Her wild-eyed glance in the butler's direction told the duke there was little time to waste. His gut twisted in a desperation he had not felt as an adult.

"In a room other than her own? Mrs. Flander, or whatever your name is, I expect you to take me to her ladyship immediately. For, if you do not, you will be sitting in Newgate before nightfall and will remain there for the foreseeable future."

"But I can't take you to her. It's unseemly."

"By all that is holy, you can, and you will."

"I can't for I do not know where she is, exactly," revealed Mrs. Flander.

The man the woman called Mr. Flander said, "She's right, milord. She was taken down to Carrington Corner. We don't know what happened to her there."

"The hell you say!" exclaimed Jasper. He turned to Richard and said ominously, "The Corner of Indiscretion."

"We left the club too soon!"

Richard took a step toward the couple and there was banging on the outer door. The front door opened just at that moment and Richard tore his eyes from the scene in front of him to lean over to see who was in the foyer.

"Hello in the house. Amesbury. Jasper. Speak up. You there?" Thayer's authoritative voice rang in the open spaces.

Richard nodded and smiled his relief. "Yes," he called down, "just the men I need. I don't know why you are here, but I am more than thankful you are." He gestured toward Jasper and the two servants or whoever they were. "I need a few to stay and help Jasper rid the house of every man, woman, and child and hold them while you search it from top to bottom. In case I am on a wild goose chase, we want them here until I have Sarah. Then we will turn them out without a copper between them. The others, if you would come with me, I'll explain on the way."

"Right. I'll have my driver follow us for the return trip. This is a pleasant way to spend an afternoon. Good to have run into you today, my friend," said O'Leary with a laugh. "Life is never boring in London."

The man was feisty and strong and loved a good rumble. Richard was glad to have him along but not glad to be the reason he was entertained today. Trenton entered Richard's carriage first, followed by Kendrick, then O'Leary. Richard instructed the driver and climbed in just as the conveyance moved. Richard immediately began to fill his companions in.

Chapter 10 Time To Save His Darling

"This is preposterous!" declared Ashton.

"This won't be allowed. We will get her back," Kendrick said with confidence.

But Richard liked O'Leary's words the best. "Your girl is a little spitfire if she allowed you to spank and then comfort her. She is not going to allow anything to happen to her without putting up a grand battle. I bet we hear her before we reach her."

"I pray you are right, O'Leary."

"Aye, and when we have her back safe and sound, I'd be teaching her another lesson about safety," said O'Leary.

Richard nodded. "Indeed."

Richard couldn't stop his heart from beating nearly out of his chest. His fear for his Darling, his princess, was more than he could even quantify at this moment. What if they were too late, and she had been harmed? There was no telling what he would do if she was hurt. If her feminine sensibilities were damaged, he would join the Scot in doing as much reciprocal injury as he could. If the men didn't survive, it would not be a substantial loss. Selling women was barbaric and purchasing them, possibly even more so.

"Griffin, we have decided that you and Kendrick will find Sarah and put her into your carriage and get her away. I will assist O'Leary. We'll take care of the two men and meet you back at Henderson House."

"Aye, and my man will jump in because he's a wild Scot too and neither of us has had a good round of fisticuffs in too long."

As they pulled onto the road that ran directly in front of the club, heading toward the corner perpendicular to that same establishment, Richard tensed as he readied to exit their carriage. The thought ran through his mind that Sarah was in danger, first from the men on the street, then from him. He refused to allow his mind to go to a place that questioned why she never told him she was alone and without protection. That was for after she was safe.

When they finally arrived at the appropriate corner, Sarah looked much worse for the wear, but she was a fighter and in that split second, Richard was proud of her. Her gown was tattered, her hair in a wildly disheveled way. In fact, the only time he had seen her hair even the slightest bit out of place was when he had her over his knee. There were smudges on her cheek, one very dark. His blood boiled.

They needed to cut off the escape of the hack that sat stopped in front of the area where Sarah was. Richard yelled out the side window to do just that and his driver, incredible man that he was, heard and pulled in front of the carriage, placing his team at an angle to the other team, blocking any movement. O'Leary's driver pulled behind the conveyance, effectively boxing the hired hack in place.

Richard observed a man pulling and pushing her into the stance that he wanted, and he watched her jerk against the manhandling. His girl was not there because she chose to be, she was being kept against her will.

Now that he was closer, he saw a third man. The odds were good. Money was changing hands as Sarah darted away. Ashton, the first out of the coach, ran in Sarah's direction but turned back and said, "Get the carriage."

At that moment, the men on the street looked up, assessed the situation, and then scattered. The man who had been holding Sarah until she broke free, brandished a knife.

O'Leary laughed loudly, sounding a bit maniacal. "Brought a knife with you, I see m'laddie. Good, so did I."

The knife that appeared from beneath his friend's coat was the size of a large butcher knife. Kendrick went for the dirty little man who had been the money handler and after two swings of the fist, his opponent was down and looked knocked out.

O'Leary had the other man subdued somehow and Kendrick was approaching the third man who had slipped in the mud. Richard took one look in the direction of Ashton, quite a distance down the road, and saw he was just catching up with Sarah. Richard jumped back into his carriage while yelling to his coachman to drive towards Lord Ashton and the lady.

The carriage pulled up next to Lord Ashton, who was muddy and looked nearly as battered and bruised as Sarah did. She was still fighting Ashton and the poor man looked at a loss as to what he should do. Richard's voice boomed across the scene.

"Sarah Morgan, stop this behavior right now."

His voice was moderate in tone but loud in recrimination. She stopped and then when Ashton would loosen his hold on her, she fought again.

"Sadie, it is me, Richard."

She stopped her struggling. "Richard?"

He slid her matted hair aside, uncovering her face to him. "Yes, princess. It's me."

The relief was a full physical relaxation of her body. Sadie fell into him as though she were unable to hold herself up and needed his assistance. He was good with that. His knees were weak at the thought of finally having her safely in his arms.

Ashton spoke to the coachman, and they climbed back into the carriage, Richard holding Sadie even though she tried to push him away.

"Stop and let me comfort you."

"I'm fine," was her brave answer as she tried to push back from him.

"Are you fine enough to feel the flat of my hand for defying me?"

She shook her head and hung it. "I'm sorry, sir," she whispered.

He drew her close again. "Lay your head back down, little one. You're safe."

When they arrived back at the corner where it all began, Ashton got out first, followed by Richard and a very reluctant Sadie. She didn't want to return to this place, nor did she want to let go of Richard.

Kendrick spoke. "I think we have the parties all identified. Pick," he indicated the young man with the knife, "is part of the Flanders group of thieves. He brought Sarah here against her will because you had insisted that she was in the house. Their intent was to strip the house of valuables once they had disposed of Sarah."

Sadie cowered behind Richard. "He has a knife," she said from her protected place with little more volume than a whisper.

"Oh, aye, he did lass, but I can promise ye he does'na have it now." O'Leary held up the knife with some pride. "It doesn't compare with me own, but my wee lass will enjoy adding it to her collection."

Richard noticed the more excited O'Leary became, the more pronounced lilt he had to his words.

"Unfortunately, the other one," Kendrick indicated off in a different direction, "took off that way. Figured he was likely just here for merchandise. Oh, and we decided to pay the hack driver and let him go on to earn his wages. It wasn't his fault the fare he acquired was a reprobate."

Richard's chest rumbled loudly with his anger. "But we shall take that one back with us."

Kendrick looked the scraggly crew up and down and then said, "Seems that you had some difficulty with the Little Darling."

Ashton looked down at himself and the others, "True, but the two of you don't look fresh from the bath either."

Kendrick laughed. "Touché."

The men turned to look at the vendor of women who had coins at his feet. He had stooped to gather them to return to his bag. When he straightened again, he looked at the well-appointed men before him and regardless of the state of their clothes and their altercation upon arrival, he perked up.

"Gentlemen, are you here to purchase this lovely woman? She's pristine if you understand my meaning," said the filthy man.

Before Richard or any of his companions could take a step forward, Sadie marched from behind her protector and yelled.

"I am not for sale, you obscene little man!"

Richard tried to restrain his lady and give her a comforting look, but she kicked his shin as though she thought him a villain. Ashton grabbed for her and held her tightly by one hand, but Sadie kicked at him as well. She missed, but he jerked and let her arm drop causing a momentary silence. Richard's expression changed to chastising. The gentlemen stood stiffer.

"Sadie. Behave and allow me to take care of this." When she was quiet, he focused his attention on the man in front of them.

Richard's words were accompanied by a look that would have withered even the strongest of men. He addressed the vendor before him. "Of what concern is that to us?"

"I thought you to be of discerning taste." The man smiled showing several missing teeth in a blackened mouth.

"And? What are you proposing?"

The peddler opened his mouth and closed it several times before actually uttering a response. He looked at all four men with doubtful eyes.

"The young lady needs stability, sir... er... sirs. I'm just helping her find it. But with four of you, I'm sure..." The man shrugged as if the selling of women was acceptable and equally acceptable if sold to one or many. "I mean, surely stability would be something you could offer. And if I'm to gain a small profit from the exchange, it is only fair."

Kendrick spoke, his voice stone cold. "Is it? Is it indeed?"

The accompanying raised eyebrow and severe countenance seem to shake the man even more.

"Then how much is she?" demanded Richard.

Sadie gasped. "I trusted you. You would purchase me? You are the lowest form of life. I abhor you!"

"Princess, I am trying to have compassion for you because you have undergone a horrific ordeal, but you need a spanking and if you utter one more word, when this is settled, I will be more than obliging, no matter the audience."

"You wouldn't dare," said Sadie with extra effort at sounding like an insulted princess.

"Aw, little one, you have trouble controlling that tongue of yours. Your papa will be quite challenged with you. It is too bad that I will now have to paddle you. Now will I have to redden your arse or only pinken it depends on if you let me handle this properly. Remember the penalty."

She opened her mouth but said nothing more. She stomped her foot and the odious man jumped to the side as though he expected her to stomp on his foot.

"Ah, so you are in the market for a delectable bit of innocence I see." The man seemed to stand a little straighter and become a little glibber. "Yes, I believe that 10 pounds would suffice." He paused and looked at the men meaningfully. "Each."

"10 pounds?"

Richard's voice seemed to shatter the ground beneath them. He looked at his girl who was shivering in fear while still able to convey her shock at the proceedings. She was his, and no one devalued his woman. He was contemplating turning O'Leary and his knife loose on the vermin. When she was his wife, there would be quite a few things she would be answering for. Her backside would be red for some time to come. He pulled Sadie in closer to him and saw the days old bruise beneath the mud.

"Hey, I brought her here. I never got my bit for that," said Pick.

"So, you are the one who hurt her? Assaulted her? Stole her from her home?"

Pick tried to back up, but the Laird wouldn't allow him to go any further. O'Leary punched him dead center of his nose. Then shook his hand.

"Bloody hell that hurt."

"O'Leary, mind Sadie's presence," said Richard.

"I forgot you English are sensitive. My Cairis is a strong talker when she has a mind. Sorry about that, Lady Sarah."

Sadie tossed both men a dissatisfied twist of her lips as she crossed her arms. "That man is trying to sell me and that is what you argue about?"

Richard ignored Sadie and spoke to the trader who was confused at the turn of events. "I'll offer you five."

"Five?" The sleazy man adjusted his amount. "Sir, the woman is surely worth more than that."

"Oh, she is," responded Ashton, "and the constable would be happy to know you asked for such a good price."

"Constable? What constable? I mean, I don't believe we need to bother another about this matter."

"Well," said Richard, having caught on to what his friend was trying to do, "We do want you to get the fairest price and I believe that asking someone in a more official capacity is the right thing to do. I have a great friend from Oxford who would make himself available to me if I asked."

Kendrick nodded. "He might be in the club across the street even now. Shall we all go, and see?"

The man sputtered. "I have another bit of business to attend to gentlemen and do not have the time to put into this exchange."

"Oh, no?" asked Richard.

The man shoved at Sadie and Kendrick standing near her. He pushed away from the group, not waiting to gather his meager bits from the space he had inhabited all day.

"Remember to not return to this corner again," said Richard.

"This street," said Ashton.

"But I live here."

Richard answered. "I suggest you move."

Kendrick looked hard at the house they had seen him emerge from and said, "I believe he is right; this is his house, but the question is, does he live here alone? In for a penny, in for a pound. I say we offer any women inside to leave with whatever they have a mind to take, if they desire."

Ashton agreed. "We had better. When one acquires a wife, they tend to upset the order of things for husbands. They are always in the save mankind, mode."

Richard and O'Leary watched the despicable man scurry off after seeing what was happening to his business. Satisfied he didn't mean to return, the men turned back to Sadie and found her energetically walking away. Richard put his long legs to work and caught up with her in seconds.

"Oh, no my girl. I mean to take you home and have a strong word with you. And then, when this is over, I plan your papa makes sure your behavior is thoroughly addressed."

Sadie placed her hands on her hips and stomped in outrage. "My behavior? My papa? You have not earned that right. I didn't ask that man to lay his hands on me, nor did I agree to his outrageous proposition. I didn't invite the Flanders back into my house. I am a victim of monstrous proportions, and you would punish me?"

Richard lifted his brow. "And yet you allowed yourself to be alone without asking the solicitor or me for help. Or any of the contacts I left you in the city. Pray tell me why that is?"

His spicy, mud-stained Darling whom Richard acknowledged was a beauty even if she was a reckless thing, had found her voice, and he was fascinated by her response. Most women of his acquaintance would have fallen into their submissive act, turned teary-eyed, and hidden any anger that they felt. Not his Little princess. She defiantly stood her ground even in the face of her obvious misstep.

He knew she was likely falling apart inside. What woman wouldn't? Her anger and misunderstanding of he and his friend's role in this entire business, however, was rather insulting. The very idea that he would be anything but protective and possessive given their extensive correspondences was unconscionable.

How he would have loved to slap her arse until she released her stubbornness and then he would kiss her and bring her to such heights of ecstasy she would float for days. But she wasn't his. Yet. And while she was still young, she was of a proper age for him to show his attention toward her.

Without even thinking, he asked, "How old are you? When is your birthday, precisely?"

She stared and her defiance lessened. "I'm not sure what business of yours that is... sir." Richard acknowledged that she was not using his given name and while in this situation he would have been fine with it, she didn't know that. "You may have saved me from having to become quite violent on the public street, but I can assure you that it does not afford you any special privileges."

"Privileges? What sort do you refer to, my princess?"

"Stop referring to me as your princess and it is an unseemly question that you ask me."

Ashton stepped closer. "I believe we need to move any further discussion from the street." He looked around him to indicate the small crowd gathering.

Richard nodded sharply and reached for the door of his coach that the driver had brought to rest beside them. Sarah turned when Richard's carriage arrived. She sent a worried look in Ashton's direction and then in Richard's. Something seemed to be causing her great distress. She knew him. Should be trusting of him after all their contact over the last few years, and yet Richard saw her debating and thinking hard for a way out of this situation.

It was possible she was fearing his retribution, or his chastisement. Possibly she was worried to return to Henderson House, but whatever the reason, they were getting inside the carriage and returning to the townhouse.

Suddenly, he realized why she didn't just accept his offer of a safe escort home. It was possible that there was more going on than he knew to have caused the situation in the first place. Did she think she was still in danger? His Darling Duchess surely couldn't fear they would return her to the Flanders without his protection. Or maybe she thought Ashton meant to do her serious harm. It was too much to untangle now.

"Do not fear me, little one. I may have designs as to your future discipline, and how you spend your days forward, but I promise you as a duke at the service of the crown, that I, nor any of my friends would ever do you mortal harm."

He watched Sadie as she contemplated his words. She looked at him, and then Ashton and now the other two men along with Pick coming in their direction, the second coach following them.

"Sadie, you know me. My designs are honorable. My love is for you and no one else. Enter the carriage, little one. Papa will take good care of you. Trust me."

She nodded and whispered her assent. He gave her a gentle smile and reached out his hand which she automatically took. He then placed his second hand at the small of her back, using light pressure to steady her and encourage her to enter.

Once seated, Richard spoke to the others and soon all had entered the carriages and were on their way back to Sadie's home where the other gentlemen should still be. Relieved that they were all on their way down the street away from their audience, Richard tried once again.

"Could you tell me what has happened since I saw you last? It appears I have missed a great many things in your letters."

She remained silent for a moment. "You can leave me anywhere that is convenient. I can find my way home." She watched as the thunderous look descended changing his countenance. "I... I mean, I've decided to find another place to live."

"Yes, well, I have a great desire to make sure my lady is well cared for and from the looks of it, she has been anything but. And who but I will battle the monsters of the world or wrap you in comforting arms when you need cuddles? Who will ensure you eat good food and not too many sweets? Or provide appropriate entertainment, fresh air, and new clothes? And who will handle your naughty behavior, I wonder?"

Richard could see the longing in her eyes and the moment she realized she was supposed to provide those things for herself. She pulled herself straighter in her seat and began to withdraw into herself. There was a pained expression, and her face twisted, but then it cleared.

He watched her rise a full two inches in angry stature. While it was cute as hell, he couldn't let her get herself further in the suds than she was already.

"I do not need those things. I am perfectly capable of providing for myself. Lord Henderson has taken care of me."

"Yes, but his intent was for you to find a husband and until you do, you had the means for the life he had groomed you to enjoy. To expect. I want to be that man for you, but we have things to settle first."

"You just want the money Lord Henderson left for me."

Ashton leaned forward and spoke in a reasonable tone. "Did you not hear that this man is a duke? He does not need your money. The Daring Duke is gifted in his business transactions. He doesn't have to waste his time on random young ladies. If he has chosen you for his duchess, then you are not insignificant, nor would I turn him down."

"Why not, pray tell? I like my freedom."

"Really? Do you really?" asked Ashton.

"I'm sure my princess doesn't mean to cause such a ruckus, and she certainly isn't being ungrateful for the rescue. She is just tired and dirty. It's been a long stressful day on top of long stressful weeks." He smoothed her unadorned hair and placed his hand on hers. "Do not be ungrateful, princess. I know what you are about, and I won't let you do it. You were raised for marriage and companionship, a papa, and independence. With me, you can have it all, but it frightens you. We shall work through it."

His tone held both indulgence and warning. Then he waited to see how she would respond.

"Months," she said.

"What?"

"It has been months since I have been cared for and secured. I have not been alone all that time, but I have been a prisoner for most of it."

Now Richard was feeling his anger rise again. He barely registered Ashton's grunt of disbelief. Richard pulled her tight to him. He would figure this out and then he would take care of his little one. There was time enough to rectify things and put their lives back in order. A new order. Sarah Morgan was his and there was no way he would ever let her go.

Chapter 11 Time for Truth

For the first time since entering the carriage, Sadie took notice of the plushness of the interior. She found the seats were made of the most buttery leather. She unconsciously rubbed her arms and within seconds, a blanket appeared. Her lord, who was now a duke, tenderly tucked it around her legs and when she should have felt scandalized, she felt warmth. It wasn't a feeling she was used to having in recent months and never to this degree, and it made her uncomfortable. When Sadie would protest, a look of chastisement from Richard made her belly clench and tingle.

"Let me take care of you until we get you home and then we will sort everything out. You must have been frightened by that unsavory incident. All the events."

She nodded. That achiness now descended deep into her nether regions. How embarrassing. It was a feeling she had not experienced before, not to this depth. The sensation was almost a pain. This whole thing must be unseemly and surely in her distorted imagination it was difficult to decide what was good and what was not. She was sure it wasn't something other women must think of. Maddeningly, she didn't seem able to turn off her thoughts. The mere image of Richard being protective and demanding was exciting. Even while Sadie hated it, she longed for it.

Richard whispered close to her ear. "I was frightened too. I couldn't imagine a life without you in it. Will you contemplate spending your days with me?"

Sadie was so enthralled in her world of what-ifs, she missed the question. There was a sudden tap on her thigh. Not painful, but attention-getting.

"Woolgathering? You will keep me alert, my dear."

The smile Richard gave her seemed scandalous. But he was, wasn't he? He was enticing and exciting.

"Sarah, are you tired?"

"Yes, so very sleepy."

She yawned. Ashton laughed. Richard smiled.

"You have had quite a day, and we are only at midafternoon. We are almost to the house. Time to put on our best face and take care of everything. Never let the world know you are distressed is a very important lesson in being a duchess," said Ashton.

Richard gave him a scowl which he promptly ignored. "Do not encourage the minx. I want her open and honest with me."

"She doesn't need anyone to tell her what she already knows. She must always be open and honest with her papa," said Richard. "It is important, and I will tolerate nothing else. Besides, like all of our women, she is quite a saucy little one all on her own."

Ashton made a pseudo bow from the bench across from Sadie causing a slight upward tilt of her lips. "I am Lord Ashton, and my wife is Rosemary. She is eager to meet you, Lady Sarah."

The man seemed much more jovial now that they would soon drop her off at her house of horrors. She mustn't let that happen.

She nodded at the man who had wrangled her improperly in the street getting them both muddy.

"I don't want to go home, sir." Her voice was clearer than she expected.

"No, I imagine you don't. But your papa will be there to protect you," said Richard.

"I don't have a papa."

"You do, and I am not in the mood to play games. I will explain all after we are through this part. Are you worried about what will happen once the complete story comes out?"

"It determines who does the telling, sir."

"I understand, but we must take care of things. It is your home, and you should be able to be comfortable and safe."

"You don't understand. I am ensuring my safety and the only way to do that is to stay away from that house. Richard, I am in danger there. They have invaded me and my peace twice.

"Sarah?"

His tone sent her hands at once clenching themselves and her thighs pressing together hard. That odd ache was back again but stronger and she had the damnable urge to stare at the floor whilst doing what the man said.

The duke turned slightly in her direction. She saw the house and panicked. Sadie instinctively knew that the man wasn't bluffing, but how could she trust him? So much had happened that trust didn't come easy anymore. She didn't know him like she thought she had before. Too much time had passed.

"Please?" she begged. "Leave me off somewhere else."

The duke seemed relaxed now, even jovial. She imagined it was because she would soon be out of his orderly life. Even though he said the right things, he had stopped correspondence after he left London when Lord Henderson died. She had needed him so much but shortly after that time, he stopped writing. How could she think it was for no other reason than his lordship had died and therefore no more pretense was needed?

They stopped at a corner waiting for carefree ladies to cross a side street before the team would go forward. In that moment of stillness, Sadie took that opportunity to leap from the carriage and head down the street. Her dress was a great hindrance, and she knew she looked a fright, but she ran. Within seconds the duke had her in his grasp. He took her back to the carriage, and she tried to yank her arms from his hold without success.

Richard leaned down and whispered harshly in her ear, "Either you get into the carriage for your own safety and under your own power or I will toss you inside and spank that plump backside so long, sitting will be a mere memory."

"Sir, you would not!"

"I assure you, princess, I would take great joy in performing that task. What is your choice?"

"But I am afraid, Richard."

"Get in and we shall decide what to do. I will protect you but the only way you will believe that, is if I do it. The only way I can show you is to actually do it."

With a great show of irritation and extreme reluctance, she allowed herself to be handed up into the carriage. The brute was quite gentle when he made sure she entered his conveyance once again.

Ashton sat down again and before Sadie could say anything, Richard settled her over his knee and smoothed her dress down over her behind. She sighed in the feeling of belonging. Her dress was rather thin, and she enjoyed the style of it but wished she had elected to wear one of Lady Henderson's dresses with much more material in the skirt.

"I require you to repeat or respond to me to show you understand the lesson. Now, repeat, I will always bring my problems to my papa."

"But..." a smack landed on her backside.

She repeated after him and then grunted when he landed several additional swats on her bottom.

"Keeping secrets is a dangerous and unseemly thing to do."

"Keeping secrets is a dangerous and unseemly thing to do. Ow! Ow! Sir!"

"I know my strength, Sadie, and it is not too much. You are able to handle so much more."

"I promise never to repeat the error of today's adventure."

When she did not respond, he landed four sharp smacks to her bottom. "Sarah, say it."

"I cannot sir."

"Why not?"

"I can't promise that. Who knows if I will need to do so to try to stay safe?"

"There will never be a time that you will be required to put yourself in danger to get yourself safe."

Richard's hand landed a flurry of spanks which she accompanied with her screeching and yells of dissatisfaction. He sat her up without a word and sat her next to him again. He immediately withdrew his hand from her side when she flinched and inhaled air through her teeth.

"What's wrong? Are you hurt? Did I hurt you?"

It seemed like a good time to make him feel bad. She didn't know what that throbbing was, but after Richard had his hand on her side, it was stinging terribly. Her hand came away with new blood.

"I... I think I'm bleeding."

Richard snatched her to him and lifted her petticoats, accompanied by her screams. "I can't... milord... Stop!"

"Sadie, I must make sure you do not require a physician. There is blood."

"We are not alone, Your Grace."

"We are not..." Richard's hand stayed. "Oh. But he is a papa and understands completely."

"Yes, sir, but he is his *wife's* papa."

"By all that is holy, woman, you're hurt."

Ashton spoke using his typical calm logic. "Griffin, we are here. Can you not take her inside and in the privacy of her room or another, do your examination, and then determine from there whether more care is necessary?"

Richard was not a man who waited when it might be harmful to do so. She had learned that about him. He looked at Sadie. "Please, milord?" She added what she was certain would change the outcome. "Please, Papa?"

His face transformed into gentle determination. "Yes, quite right. Apologies, Ashton."

That man merely dipped his head the slightest bit in acknowledgment. Sadie felt lips touch her mussed, dirty hair, and that scandalized her more than his demonstrative behavior.

"Your Grace!"

"My apologies again. I don't know what has come over me."

Richard spoke but Sadie heard no real remorse and if one were to look into his heart, she was sure they'd find none. He was a man very sure of his world. She wished she was.

"Yes," answered Ashton, "We should exit the carriage before you lose your mind and do something the lady's reputation will not recover from."

Sadie laughed sardonically. "That ship has sailed, milord."

Richard nodded. "So, it has."

Richard seemed determined to keep hold of her hand and while his grasp was a bit too tight, she didn't want to consider the alternative. She didn't want to imagine what would now happen. It was scary seeing the Flanders again or whoever they were. She wondered if she could sell the home she loved so much to purchase another? She would be heartbroken but now that this place held such dreadful memories, she could feel herself tremble at the thought of being alone brought her. even now.

Sadie looked over at Richard Griffin, the Duke of Amesbury, and shook her head. He was so handsome and powerful, surely, he didn't mean it when he told her he wanted her to be his. Would he want her to be his wife? And what of his family? They would not allow it. He was a very rich and influential man according to Lord Henderson. He couldn't want to keep her with him. It was impossible.

She resolved that he would release him from his rash words. His letters were full of the future and dreams of sharing his with her. She was fanciful to have ever thought he was serious or that even if he was, when the reality of the classes was pushed on him, he would leave her to find her way so she had better make sure she could do it now.

Sadie raised her head and stiffened her spine. Time to face the events of the day. If there was a clear victim, it was her but did her actions of trying to handle things herself cause this to happen? Was it her fault? What did her duke think?

Sadie didn't lean into Richard as she instinctively wanted to do. She heard him sigh and didn't force her to do so, for which she was grateful. If he exerted his natural commanding nature on her, she would have crumbled, her resolve lost. Instead, Richard took her hand and led her up the steps. Her side stung but not as much as her nose and eyes. She would not cry.

She was ushered inside and there were several men she thought she might have met on another night long ago, like Lord Ashton, but she couldn't recall because all she saw was Lord Griffin, her duke. The men were sitting and having a drink, conversing as though she hadn't just had the very worst day of her life. As Ashton preceded her and Richard into the room, things grew silent for a few seconds and then every man took to his feet.

Richard's warmth drew her close and his breath warmed her suddenly cold face. "Let me introduce you quickly and then I shall escort you to your chambers to see to the wound."

"No. May I not simply clean up a bit and put on clean clothing? It would be easier to meet gentlemen with a little more dignity, sir. Please. Embarrassment at the situation I have found myself in is monumental already."

"Agreed. But I will accompany you." Sadie opened her mouth and Richard leaned closer to her ear, "Not negotiable. You are no longer free to do as you wish no matter the consequences, my princess. You are mine to protect and I do not intend to let you out of my sight."

Richard said a few words to the men in the room and just as he was ushering her to the staircase, Pick, and his guards arrived. Richard directed them to the parlor and led her to the stairs. As they gradually climbed the staircase, Sadie's side began to ache and pull. It felt like it was tearing. Likely it had opened again. The liquid she knew was blood was dripping down her outer leg. It had her full attention now, and she worried she had done herself real harm. She slowed her ascent to give the area less stress. Suddenly she screeched when she was swooped up into strong, masculine arms.

"Milord, I am fully grown. *Your Grace!*" she hissed. "People will see," she whispered.

"Yes, I am quite aware of that, princess. I am also aware that your side hurts, and the grimace on your face gave away the level of pain. I am your papa, and I am perfectly within my rights to see to your injuries, your comfort, and your health, among many other things. You have not ever had a papa or even a proper father, so you are not to know. You have, however, had benefactors and kind people in your life that have taken you under their wing and protected you. I am so much more than that."

"I don't understand."

"No, my Little Darling, I am sure that is true. I am equally sure your reputation will never recover so you may as well consent to marry me. Let us sort things out today and then I will begin to explain and teach you what all this means to you, and to us. Can you trust me?"

Sadie knew trust wasn't the real dilemma, it was when he discovered she wasn't what he had hoped. She wasn't a lady, but he knew that. What he didn't know was that she only knew what she had been taught. It wasn't ingrained. It wasn't who she was from birth. Wasn't that obvious to those, like his family, who were born to the manor?

She had benefactors, but she had no parents, no lineage, and no prestige associated with her name. She had a dowry, yes, but turning her money over to a man she was positive would soon be ashamed of her, was not going to happen. If he stayed after committing to her and sealing their alliance and producing an heir, possibly she could trust him. Was it fair to him? Possibly not, but she had to be cautious.

"How do you know where my room is?"

"Oh, my dear, I have as much a story to tell as you, but first we will find out why you are bleeding and what I should do to make you feel better."

He sat her down and Sadie turned to close the door in anticipation of Richard leaving the room. "I can handle things on my own."

"I am not at all comfortable leaving you where you are not properly supervised or cared for. I am certainly not allowing you to deal with blood and in the absence of another female, you will settle with me."

"I can assure you that I am a grown woman. I do not need supervision. I need to be allowed to deal with things my own way. Without you." She softened her tone. "I am eternally thankful that you have taken an interest in me over the years. It was exhilarating for a young girl with no hopes of a good marriage or even a decent place in society to have such a man of prestige to pay me visits."

"Did you hit your head? Are you feeling unwell?"

This was harder than she thought. Sadie took a slow, deep breath and released it.

"You made my imagination soar, but I am fully adult now, with no benefactor and no one to put pressure on you to share time with me. My childish dreams have been put away. I release you from any obligations you may have had toward me. Please take your friends, and if you would leave the Flanders to the constabulary on your way home, that will end your obligation towards me."

He seemed shocked. "Your blood loss cannot be so severe that you would speak this gibberish."

She nearly pleaded with him to leave. "Please tell them I am eternally thankful. It's time I take over my life and find a husband who will be satisfied with what I have to offer him."

Richard's face reddened. "Are you implying, no, accusing me of not appreciating you? Not cherishing you? Of doing this due to pressure placed upon me? Obligation?" His voice grew more aggravated.

"No, I'm releasing you from any misguided obligation. I know you meant well, and I am eternally grateful, but I understand and now I am liberating you from any perceived duty."

"You will not say those things to me."

His frustration was great but so was Sadie's. Even though she understood that he thought it improper, what was she to do? And how was she to stop him from entering her life if he demanded it? Sadie needed him with every fiber of her being, but she would not accept him out of his misplaced sense of responsibility.

It was true. She was unprotected and unprepared for the world she had been plunged into. Lord Henderson was trying to do what he thought was right for her but maybe it was Lady Henderson who had the right of it all along. She didn't have what a husband of means and position required and to raise her hopes, while unintentional, was cruel. There was no one to save her from who she was or to change society as a whole. No, better he left now. She couldn't bear to see him grow to despise her.

"I don't want you here."

Richard laughed. Laughed! Sadie stood tall and regal in her filthy kitten slippers and her bedraggled appearance. Five feet four inches suddenly didn't seem as significant as previously thought.

"We will tease all of this out, I promise you. Let us see what has hurt you, change your clothing, and clean your face. The gentlemen downstairs will need to get back home soon."

He picked her up gently, moved her further into her room, and began to unbutton her dress. Sadie stepped out of his way and stomped her foot.

"I will undress myself. Please leave me to it."

"After that speech you just delivered, do not expect me to leave you alone for a very long time. I assure you that you have done nothing more than ensure my presence. Now, either you allow me to undress you, or I will lay my hand to your backside again and then undress you. Which shall be your choice?"

She swung her foot and then stomped. "Oh!"

"And the next time you stamp your foot at me, princess, or try to kick me because you are not getting your way, I will lay my leather across your sit-upon. Is that understood?"

She stared at him. "Yes, I understand." She felt a hard swat on her backside. "Sir."

Richard nodded. "I know you are scared, tired, and misinformed just for starters, but we have things to do and then we can begin to put life back in clear view. Lift your arms."

She did as he asked without thinking. Her shift covered the most delicate of places on Sadie and she had so many conflicting emotions she wanted to scream. Richard's face hardened as he looked at her.

"You are displeased with me."

"Yes, I am displeased but not with you. I am displeased because you have dried blood in a path down your leg. You have finger marks on your arms, you have a dark bruise on your face and your shift is blood-stained. I fear what I may see beneath. Lift your shift."

"Richard..."

"Sadie, Papa said lift your shift."

"Your Grace..."

"Now, Sarah."

Sarah. Was that what he would call her when she was disobedient or slow to respond to his commands? She hated it with her mind and yet tingled in the depths of her body. She was a disaster. Sadie lifted her shift quickly to get the action over with. He took it off over her head and since the petticoats were gone with the outer dress she stood before him without anything to cover her. She didn't wear a corset. It was a torture device that she refused to wear once Lady Henderson died.

"You are wonderfully made. Your body is perfect, but right now, that perfect body has a cut. How did that... did the man who stole you do this to you?"

"I wasn't... compliant." She stole a glance at her side and saw the neat slice across her side.

She was certain he swore under his breath but being brought up to be a gentleman, he wouldn't curse in front of her for it was crass and impolite. Sadie rather liked hearing it sometimes. Another testament to her lack of ladylike skills.

There was a knock at her door. Jasper was at the entrance with a pitcher of warm water. "The tea water that was decided against. She can use it to cleanse the wound and other places."

"Thank you, my friend. We will be down soon."

Richard closed the door and poured some water into the basin and washed her face first. Once he had washed enough, he tossed the water out the window and poured more to wash the wound and saw the blood made it look much worse than it was.

"See, nothing to be concerned about," said Sadie as she looked at the cleansed area.

"Someone hurt you and that is of grave concern to me." He poured some of the water into her wash basin and cleansed the rest of her body of blood and debris. "You will need it to be stitched but only a couple."

"No. That will hurt."

"Only for a moment but you cannot leave this open because it will not heal well. I'll be with you."

"No."

Richard sighed. "We will discuss it."

He found a handkerchief and long hair ribbons that he tied around her waist and over the folded material for a bandage until he could get her to a physician.

"I won't change my mind," she said.

"Sarah, love, let me wash your arms, and let us find you a loose gown."

She could agree to that. After Richard gently washed all the remaining dirty bits and helped her to do up the buttons on her heavier gown with an ample flowing bodice and skirts, he grabbed a knitted sweater and a clean pair of slippers of similar color before leading her out of the bedroom.

"Now we will find out the whole story of what happened today."

Richard sounded resigned and Sadie understood the feeling. He led Sadie out to meet the group of men she had gotten a glimpse of on her way into the house. She hoped she could get through this without offending anyone and still come away with minimal heartache.

Chapter 12 Time for These Feelings He Evokes

Sadie was sure she was losing her faculties. Her mind must be going crazy because everything that she had always wanted: independence, stability, the right to make her own decisions, and the wherewithal to accomplish those dreams and choices was hers. And when she had been given all of that, she had opened her door to the Flanders. Then they opened the door for themselves, and she had been powerless to remove them.

She was frightened and at that moment three days ago when she knew she couldn't get rid of the Flanders, she wished it all away. She had feared for her life, really feared for the first time in her existence. It was even worse than when she lost her mother because she knew she had a place to be and people around her that would make sure she was cared for. Not now. She was alone.

There were the Arnolds, and they were incredible people, but they had their own lives and lived in another place. If her duke hadn't arrived with his friends, she would have likely been dead or worse by now and not a soul would have noticed. Well, at some point Mr. Shackelford would have inquired and the Arnolds would have come by eventually, but it would be to naught.

The tears slid down her face as she thought of the horror she encountered. She would have returned the independence, freedom of choice, the money if she could have the security of protection and a place where others around her could be trusted. Richard said he was her papa, and she wasn't sure what that meant, but what she wouldn't do for an actual protector. She longed for that blanket of safety, but he wasn't there because he wanted to be, he was fulfilling his promise to Lord Henderson. Something she could not allow him to do.

When Lord and Lady Henderson began taking an interest in Sadie, she had experienced some meanness and some jealousy, but Mr. Arnold had set them right. The staff soon settled down to life with a child that was now doted on by people of means, but no blood connection. Her last link to her blood family had been severed and lost forever with the death of her mother.

When they entered the parlor, Sadie took a step closer to Richard as she looked at the room full of powerful men. Richard was strong. He could pick her up without a thought. At first it frightened her but then it thrilled her. He was sterner than Lord Henderson, but there, beneath the no-nonsense exterior, he was a soft bunny rabbit, soft and squishy like the one he had given her.

He was making sure she had all she needed. Richard had shown that he could be watchful, protective, possessive, and demanding and it felt so good it scared her in a different way. Her intimate areas tingled, and her belly had a gnawing type of sensation. The way she had caught him looking at her and the liberties he took with her, like dressing her cut and being angry that Pick had hurt her, confused her. She wasn't anything to him. And yet, he was truly concerned.

Richard's words broke through Sadie's thoughts. She found herself sitting, and she'd no recollection of taking a seat. "Sarah Morgan, I would like to introduce you to my friends. The man who looks so happy is Lord Trenton. He is newly married. The man next to him that looks anything but happy is Lord Jasper. He is unmarried and missing his afternoon entertainment at the horse track."

"Not true, Lady Morgan. I begrudge nothing if it has saved you any hardship." Jasper took a dramatic bow.

"So gallant, milord. I am truly grateful. To all of you."

Richard introduced the established eldest of their group, Lord Thayer, the most refined in a Londoner kind of way, Lord Ashton, Lord Kendrick, the undisputed ruler of the estates, and the brash but endearing and very entertaining Scot, Laird O'Leary. He, like the others, had dipped his head in a bowing gesture of greeting. She felt a little like the princess Richard called her.

"And now, I am sorry to be the one to start with unpleasantness, but what shall we do with these Flander people," said Kendrick.

"I don't believe they are all related," said Sadie.

"No, I agree," said Lord Thayer. "We have observed them and there is no companionship as one would have in a family, even the most unconnected of families have a type of bond. Dysfunctional, but one, nonetheless. This group is likely a ragtag group of people working together for a common goal."

"Yes," spat Richard, "money and thievery."

"It is getting later in the day, and I need to return to the house if I'm to have you lot in my home to entertain this evening," announced the Laird. "So, I've no issue with dropping these miscreants off at the magistrates on my way if we have them tied up proper and tight."

"I'd like to just drop them into the sea," said Richard.

"Oh, yes. Brilliant."

Kendrick looked at Lord Ashton and shook his head. Ashton was being facetious. Richard was not.

"Yes, yes, but we could do something very similar to that. We can take them to the docks and offer them a choice: a trip to America or Jamaica or go to Newgate prison."

Sadie reached up and touched Richard's coat tail. He responded immediately by turning into her and leaning down to ask, "Are you well dear? In pain?"

"I'm not sure you can force someone to leave the country, Richard."

"You could but it wouldn't be right, I agree. We are merely proposing options of which they deserve none. A free ride to another place instead of Newgate is generous. I daresay, most would take them straight to prison."

"I suppose, but what if they return? Book a passage back? I can't deal with them a third time. I simply cannot."

His hand smoothed her hair and smiled. "Your papa is going to take care of you now, but they will have to work long and hard to afford a return passage and since, as I suspect, they are not all related, they will likely part company."

She hesitated and then nodded resolutely. "Then we must hope that they accept the passage to another place."

"That's my princess."

He straightened as two of his friends went to bring the hoodlums back into the parlor. Lined up, they were a disheveled and disgruntled lot, but Sadie imagined they were imagining the riches they could have walked away with, versus what was going to happen to them. Everything this group had forced her to do had looked to be a fate worse than death for her earlier in the day. Now, it appeared to be a fate not quite as terrible but not what they had hoped, at any rate. They had earned this result; she had not earned their conniving ways.

Richard spoke but all the men were standing. Sadie saw the Laird was playing with his knife in what appeared to be an absentminded way, but she knew he was doing it as a warning.

"We've decided to be generous and give you a choice as to your fates. Be thankful it isn't just me who decided because I would have dropped you into the middle of the Thames and walked away."

"Right then," continued Lord Thayer. "You can go on a ship to America, Jamaica, or go to Newgate prison. It is your choice, but a choice must be made. If naught is agreeable, we will take you to Newgate. We all have quite influential people associated with that place who will make sure you don't enjoy your long stay there. We have but to send a message. You will find your way in the other places but at least all speak English, for the most part. So, decide."

Kendrick pulled out his watch and tapped it lightly. "We've about three hours until the ship sailing to America leaves and ten until the ship sailing to Jamaica sails. Newgate would like us there by six p.m. if we are coming."

Richard looked at the wall behind the Flander group because he wanted to burst out laughing. There was no deadline for Newgate. They usually got them early in the day or late at night according to an acquaintance of his that declared he would have reason to know. But putting pressure on them to make a choice was fine with Richard. He wanted them gone and however that happened, it happened.

Ultimately, all chose America, thinking that the Colonies would have more to offer them. They might be right, but they would be the ones at a disadvantage. Ashton and O'Leary had shared what it was like in the Colonies and it was harder work than in England. Richard watched Sadie as her relief that the Flanders were leaving and would not have access to her or her home settled in on her. He then watched as the realization that it meant she would be alone, also descended.

"Come over tonight. Stay the night. The women will take care of the little one's cut, introduce themselves to her, and ye'll get a fine meal. Cairis has a grand cook she brings from home. Ye'll be impressed and well satisfied," said the Laird.

Richard looked at Sadie and then pulled out his watch to gauge the time. "Anyone else but this group there?"

"Nay. I've no stomach for anyone else. Besides, I imagine the lass has had enough of worry for now."

"Then we shall be there. I don't think a pub would do her tonight and I've no hand at cooking."

Sadie said, "I can cook on a spit; however, I don't choose to do so often." The men chuckled as they ushered the Flanders out under protest.

"And now you shan't have to worry about them again, my dear," assured Richard.

"We've already taken everything out of their pockets and bags that was not theirs. If Lady Morgan could look and see if there is anything on this table that is not hers, we would be happy to return it to the scoundrels." Lord Trenton pointed to the table in the entryway.

Sadie was appalled at all they had uncovered. "They must have a key to every room that is locked."

Richard smiled and reached for the chatelaine attached to Mrs. Flander or whatever her name was. It was such a common item on women, he never thought of the ring of keys attached.

Sadie nearly snatched the accessory from Richard's hand. "That was Mrs. Arnold's chatelaine that Lady Henderson gave her. She must have thought it was to stay with the keys. It was not."

She pulled out a few trinkets she did not recognize and since they were of no intrinsic value, Trenton returned them to the group. Making sure they each had a blanket, some food rations to add to the rations on the ship, their few bags, and the few coins between them that would be needed on their first days back on land, they were herded toward the door. It wasn't much money, and they would soon find out that it held little value where they were going. Hard work was what the colonists valued.

WHEN ALL WERE GONE from the house, Sadie turned and began to gather what was on the table.

"Leave it for now. Tomorrow we will find some staff for you if you wish, but for the rest of today, we will rest, talk, and plan. How is your pain?"

"I'm fine. You can go about your business, Richard. I am not an invalid nor soft-minded. I can handle life and while it doesn't look like it, I truly believe that I was an easy target because of my grief. The Arnolds will be happy to help me find more. They had helped me before, but no one wanted to work in a home with no males. It was annoying but there it is. They will keep looking if I ask."

"The Arnolds. Would they return to run this house?"

Sadie shook her head. "They are happy where they are."

"And they told you this?"

"No, but they do seem happy."

"Tell me where they are, and I will ask them to consider it."

"Demand, you mean."

He reached out his hand and caressed her cheek. "Sarah, I am an honorable man, and I would force no one to do what they chose not to do. I am also a man of obligation, but some things cannot be dictated solely by society's need to control another's behaviors. I am not that man to be dictated to nor do I follow in a direction that my gut doesn't agree, and it is telling me to ask for the Arnolds and to ask you to allow me to court you."

"I don't need saving, Your Grace."

"Sarah Morgan, I am not saving you, I am doing this for me, and if, in the process, you benefit, all the better. What do you think, my princess, can we discuss it?"

Richard wanted to take Sarah and wrap her in cotton wool for safety. Then, only for his pleasure, he would unwrap her so he could gaze at her beautiful body and listen to her sassy mouth so he could spank her, cuddle her, make love to her, and rewrap her in the cotton wool. He'd never felt this way about a woman before. Sarah was the very Darling he needed to complete him in his life.

Marriage with Sarah Morgan was now his goal for his future. Unlike a business transaction, it was his only way to contentment. He needed to have Sarah with him. Little Sadie was confused and scared, looking for comfort and unable to allow herself the freedom to ask for what she desired. That would change.

The adult woman held onto that vulnerable side of her, holding on tightly because she feared great harm if she allowed her Darling side out into the ignorant world. But with a papa, him as her papa, she would blossom. She needed him as much as he needed her, but getting her to understand and accept that fact was proving to be a challenge.

She believed, if he interpreted her words and actions correctly, that he wrote to her, visited her, and sent treats and presents to her because Lord Henderson had been his friend, and he wanted to please him. What his little princess didn't realize was that Lord Henderson denied him the thing he had most wanted more than a year ago.

Richard had written to Henderson and had asked if he could court Sarah. He wanted to offer for her hand in marriage. The man denied him even though, in reality, he had no say in whether or not Sarah was wed. Henderson was his friend, and he had always been someone Richard had looked up to when he had no father to fill the gap.

The men had several heated arguments about that very thing, but the stubborn man held Richard off. His friend was gone now, God rest his soul, and there was nothing and no one to stand in the way of marrying Sarah. Except for Sarah herself.

Henderson had even alluded in his letters that he had made a mistake and wished he'd made a different choice early on. But it was done, and Richard didn't hold grudges. He would have his Darling Duchess and it didn't matter that she came from less than a stellar background.

He would surround her with his friends' Little ladies and Darlings and that would clear the way for her to enjoy the life she wanted whether it be in society or simply on their estate. The next matter before him was to get rid of the Flanders, then get his Sarah safe and under his protection. That would be a tougher challenge than the Flanders had been, for Sarah was stubborn. He would try giving her the choice she demanded.

Richard led her to the sofa and sat, bringing her down to sit thigh to thigh. He had wanted to bring her to his lap but thought it might scare her and that was not his intention. He wanted to reassure her, convince her, make her understand his motives were his alone. That couldn't be done from his lap, yet.

Sadie nodded and pulled her tightly clasped hands into her lap. Richard put his larger, warmer hand over her chilled ones. She shivered.

He kept his voice quiet. Kind. Gentle. It wasn't what he wanted to do right now. What his instinct pushed him to do was take charge, fix her whole world in a day or even less, and live well for the rest of their lives. He had resources in his possession that would put everything to rights quickly. But his Sadie was overwhelmed, and her thoughts were making her more frightened and leading her to misinterpret everything. That was the primary thing he had to focus on first.

"I need to hear your words, little one. Papa will not assume you understand because it risks your trust in me and mine in you. So, are you ready to discuss it?"

"I do not believe there is anything to discuss, sir."

"And maybe there is where we start."

Chapter 13 Time For Change

Sadie thought if he wanted to discuss things, she would put all her cards on the table. It was a gamble, and she had already alluded to most of what she thought, but if that wasn't enough, she would make him see that being with her was a risk he didn't want to take. Then he would leave her to her own devices. She would get on with finding a husband that was not a lord, or above her station. Well, maybe a little.

"Then get on with it so you can go to be with your friends."

"Do not speak with sour notes. I am here with you because I choose to be."

"We will see."

He raised his brows to sharp peaks. "We shall see indeed. But be forewarned my little one, that snarky disrespect will get you spanked once we have established the rules."

"Rules only apply if you have dominion over me and that will never happen. I will never give over my power again. I have learned what that gets me. I will not invite trouble to my doorstep again."

"You did not know the Flanders were trouble until they showed their true colors. Submitting yourself to a worthy caretaker, me, will keep you safe and happy."

"One would think but, in my experience, —"

"In your very limited, skewed experience. Your trust was not always placed well, and the outcome was equally unpleasant. But remember, Lord and Lady Henderson and the Arthurs were very trustworthy. The Flanders were not. You are more likely to avoid those like the Flanders."

Sadie whispered at the realization of the magnitude of the Flanders' deceit and how frightened she was. How dangerous it was for her to be alone. "I can't risk my safety again. I cannot tell who is trustworthy and who is not."

"I agree. That is why you need me to take care of that for you."

He kissed the top of her head and settled his chin in the same spot. It was then that Sadie realized Richard had slowly pulled her deep into his arms. She wasn't just in his lap which was completely inappropriate, but she was now snuggled down as though she were a child, and he was her... papa.

Not a father, for she equated Mr. Arnold and Lord Henderson as surrogate fathers. They were instructive, firm, and indulgent but never anything like what she was experiencing now, with Richard.

"Sadie, you once trusted me. What changed your opinion?"

She shrugged still cradled against him. She absently played with his jacket buttons. "You stopped writing to me. Lord Henderson was taken ill so suddenly and then he was gone. I thought you would write me after leaving. I thought after we met for the two seasons that you were in London, that you would write me more often or at least keep up the amount you wrote. But after Lord Henderson died, and my life changed forever, you never wrote again."

"My poor Sadie. That is why you had the fool notion that I only paid you attention because of Lord Henderson. He was gone, and you assumed I felt my obligation was over. Although, why you would think I felt obligated to give you my attention because of him, I'll never know. He was my friend in that he received my allegiance, but he was not my master."

"I thought no one of your social standing would have given so generously of their time to spend with me unless coerced or entreated to do so."

"Your opinion of yourself is deplorable and something we shall take up later. Sadie, I wrote at Christmastide because I had hoped you would be with me soon. However, when I returned on the last trip my year of mourning was not yet over, and I couldn't subject my mother and sister to joyful events when still grieving the loss of my father.

But when I knew we were soon ending that period, I wrote and asked you to come to me. I also sent a letter to Lord Henderson. I assume it never arrived, or he was already taken ill. Sadie, I didn't write again because, other than rumors I had only heard days before, I had no idea Henderson had passed until I received the letter from Shackleford. I was waiting for you to decide on my request and was devastated when there was not a return reply."

"I never received any letter."

"I realize that, and I didn't receive Henderson's reply until after he had passed. The very next day, I received the letter from the solicitor. I received another upon my arrival to London, saying what he had already told me in previous correspondence."

"I don't want to give up my autonomy, but I am afraid to do something so simple as hire staff. And I don't want to stay completely alone. I cannot go places without an escort or companion for not only is it unseemly, but it is dangerous and yet, the actual going and coming is not frightening to me. I do not want to be your wife if by doing so, my freedoms are taken, if my life becomes a drudgery of expectations and no choices."

Her response had been bold. Too bold? Was he leaving now that she had openly defied him? Would he feel she had disrespected his question? Him? No, this one would stay because she had done worse to him this very day, and he drew closer instead of withdrawing. He confused her.

It was going to be a challenge because he was used to being right. She was used to submitting. It was expected that she would comply with him and those of his ilk, but she now had enough wealth, thanks to Lord Henderson, to walk away. But did she have the strength?

It would take all she had to walk away and refuse him but a greater strength to yield and accept him, trust his words. She wasn't sure she could do that. Trusting herself was difficult after her colossal misjudgment of character thus far. And in the presence of his powerful personality and confidence, her own wavered.

"I'm sure that you would not be happy with me, milord. I tend to have a sharp tongue."

Richard laughed, a deep throaty sound with melodic notes of confidence. "You do, but I find it adds to your charm. I saw earlier that you still have the cotton and fur rabbit I gave you."

"Bunny? Yes. I love her."

"That is also part of your charm. You can be a child who enjoys the simple frivolities of life without the trappings of adult restrictions. That is a gift you possess. I think that is the freedom you seek."

Sadie sat as tall as she could and would have slid off his lap if his hold did not tighten. "I am not a child."

"No, nor did I say you were one. I said you could be *like* one in your enjoyment. It is a gift, not something to be ashamed of. You wish for cuddles sometimes. You want structure and protection for your sense of security. There are some things, like belonging to someone who will take care of you and the trappings of life for a time, when you have had enough of being in charge. I am that person for you. I need to be needed. It is important that the people I love be reliant on me. I'm not sure why it fulfills me, but your gift endows me with deep satisfaction."

She tried again to slide off his lap and received a smack on her thigh for her trouble. Her hand went to that spot to comfort, and he snagged her hand and held it in his. His lips caressed her fingers. "No rubbing when you have been chastised. Do not attempt to get up again without permission."

Her belly flipped and her intimates were positively throbbing. Her breasts were tingling and achy. What is it that he did to her? And why did she want more? It wasn't right. He must have some type of hold on her, and she tried to push it away, but her body was resistant.

"I do not need someone else to do my tasks. I am perfectly capable of caring for myself, I do not require you or anyone else to take over. Nor do I desire anyone to smack my bottom." She stopped herself from rubbing her leg. "Or other spots. No chastisements."

But she found she couldn't look at Richard for deep in her being she knew she wanted that. Even if she could do things herself, she wanted to be able to do exactly as he had said, turn the responsibility over for a time. But only when desired. Just because she offered to turn the reins over to another occasionally did not mean she wanted to submit.

"You can be the lady of the house and still hand me your tasks for a time, when you need to. That sharing of responsibility is not something done in the open. The cuddling and submission to your papa is done in chambers, not in parlors."

"It is unseemly to be so demonstrative."

He smiled and pulled her deeper into his lap. She resisted and then relaxed. "In private, my dear, there is so much more familiar behavior and I promise you will enjoy it. Long for it and sometimes, even beg for it."

She straightened. His tone deepened. "Do not fight my hold, little one. Papa is no longer allowing your defiance."

And that was the way she wanted it. *Submit* the whispering voice in her head told her. Her thoughts were now united. This is what she wanted, security. She knew Richard and knew his character. He was a duke, and he wanted her. It was not behavior society would deem appropriate, she knew that, but if he was willing and she was willing, then why should they not give in and marry? Why should they not have a life that fulfills them?

Marry. That was a huge undertaking that she was not sure she would be able to do well. And his mother and sister, what would they think of her? Was this even right for her to allow him to put himself in the sights of gossiping men and women? Would she be able to handle life if his mother scorned her? Would his sister rebuff her offers of friendship? Before she could think, she spoke.

"What of your family?"

"What of my family? I am the head of my household. My sister is in pursuit of a husband, and I believe my mother is as well. They will be happy for me and love you."

She had hoped he would also say he loved her but, one knew that romance was not the reason most married. She had only hoped to grow fonder of her husband over time and she was already fond of Richard. It would be fine.

Sadie looked at her hands and said, "I will do it."

Silence reigned for several moments. It was quiet for so long that Sadie peeked up at Richard to see if he had heard her. He had a smile on his face and seemed to be waiting her out.

"Did you hear me, sir?"

"I heard you plainly if you mean that you just agreed to be my wife."

She shrugged. "Is that agreeable?"

He answered her by cupping her face and holding her in place while his head descended. She tried to pull back. "Be still my Sarah who would be called Sadie. I am going to kiss you."

"Sir, I don't believe it is allowed."

"Oh, it is, and more when we are married. For now, I will be satisfied with a kiss but no less."

Sadie watched his head lower and slowly touch his lips to hers. She had never kissed and wondered how many he had kissed before her. As though he could read her thoughts he raised just enough to speak. His lips touched hers as he spoke.

"Sarah, my love, open your mouth and stop thinking about anything except that your betrothed is sealing our engagement with this kiss."

All she could do was close her eyes and part her lips. The rest was magic and beyond her control to stop. She was going to burst with feelings. What did this mean? It was something she had never experienced before. But this wasn't melancholy it was exuberance. Exciting, frightening, and oh-so good. She hoped he kissed her often before all thoughts turned off.

He lifted his head and she gasped for air. "We need to practice this skill, my dear. You can breathe when we kiss."

"I couldn't think, sir, I'm not sure breathing was a possibility."

"It is as you will soon see. However, we have lounged here long enough, princess. It is time we prepare for our dinner this evening."

"Must we go? You can go and I'll stay here. Surely you don't want me to hinder your visit." She took a glance outside, and the darkness was descending.

"And stay alone all night? Oh, no. You have put yourself in my hands and I will take you with me. You are not to stay alone ever again. We do not have to stay overnight at O'Leary's place if that disturbs you. I'm not far from here. The staff should have cleaned and stocked well enough for us to stay. We could walk but since my coachman is likely in your kitchen, I'll have him take us to Dwyer House, the one that I have let for the season, and we will dress there. Go and find all you need. Tomorrow we will consider what is to be done here. Shackleford had apprised me of the state of your affairs in general. You can inform me of the particulars tomorrow."

"I truly don't mind staying here, sir."

"No prevarication. It will not be tolerated."

"No, sir. I suppose I wouldn't like it entirely, but I can do it. If I must, I can endure most things for a short time at least."

"I don't intend that you should need to endure most things any longer, my love, except for those things I ask of you."

"And what would those things be, sir?"

"That is a discussion for another time, princess. Let us go and see if we may stay at my house or if we shall need to play beggar. And not another word about staying here alone. I won't have it and you do not want it."

Richard walked the main floor and then the second floor while Sadie decided what she would wear for dinner and the next day. Nightwear. She was mortified just thinking of undressing in the duke's home or anyone's not her own.

She had never done so. Even the dressmaker came to Henderson House when something new was desired.

"Come along, Sadie. Let us see what you have chosen so we may go. I promise we will return tomorrow with a solid plan of action."

"Richard, I want to be part of the decisions about Lord and Lady Henderson's house."

"Yes, I expect you do, and I think that would be a good exercise for you, however, that is tomorrow's business. Dinner and friends are tonight's business. I am famished. It feels like a lifetime since I have eaten."

"Yes, I am rather hungry."

Richard's voice sharpened as though the concern was something new and the answer imperative. "When did you last take a meal?"

"Um, do you know, I'm not quite sure."

"I know you missed tea."

"Possibly yesterday's as well, but I did have breakfast."

Richard grunted. "Show me your choices." He reviewed Sarah's clothing as she blushed, her face turning very heated. With an approving nod, he closed the trunk and lifted it by the end strap with one hand. He left it outside her chambers before pulling the door shut. Walking down the staircase, he spoke to his coachman, a strapping man with kind eyes who headed back up to retrieve the truck.

Richard helped Sadie on with her coat, making sure all buckles and buttons were securely closed before donning his own. "Breakfast?"

"Of a kind, sir."

Sarah ducked her head and was glad they were moving outside. She turned to put her key in the lock and Richard took the bit of iron from her and secured the door. She busied herself getting into the carriage, accepting the driver's assistance. It was the same coach that brought her home earlier. She primped and rearranged her skirts as Richard entered.

Now that he had mentioned food, she was ravenous but feared what he would say if she told him, it had been just a bit of dinner the night before since she had eaten anything besides her fingernails.

"Sarah, explain what that means concerning breakfast?"

"I didn't have time."

"Remember what papa said about untruths."

His tone was so deep it sent chills up and down her spine so intense she shivered.

"It is the truth. The Flanders drug me all over the house looking for bits of treasure. I, of course, had followed his lordship's instructions and put whatever he had not hidden, in the places he had instructed me. They promised to allow me to eat when I had shown them all there was to show. I pointed out the things his lordship had told me were of some value if his brother or others wanted the expensive things. They would be satisfied, said Lord Henderson, and I would do as I saw fit with the rest."

They arrived at the townhouse Richard had rented for the season. "Yes, it appears the house is ready for us. Tomorrow, we shall acquire a maid and footman for you and a housekeeper. We shall spend time cataloging all the valuables after that and work out what to do from there and yes, you will assist me. I should also bring in my clerk that I use when here."

"Is it wise that others know about what is in his lordship's house?"

The duke had little compunction as he seemed to take over things. Sadie found she had no qualms about allowing him to do so. She did trust him, having accepted he had written her, and she did not receive it. The post was always getting lost along its route. That one bit of explanation helped her immensely.

"I am only using my trusted people. It is important to get an accounting of the resources that are now yours. Then we will decide what is best for handling and protecting those possessions. Are you agreeable?" She didn't answer at first. "Sadie?"

"Yes? I was thinking about hard it will be to allow you to take over. It was proving to be an overwhelming task. One I thought I could never attempt to undertake after those horrid people took over my life but now that I am, I don't truly want it all. I am a mess."

"We will not speak of them again except with derision. We have so much to do, our days will be full, and I want to teach you all about your new life in the evenings. My sister and mother will adore you." Sadie was not entirely sure about that.

Richard helped her out of the carriage, fed her a tea that would keep the wolf away from them both until dinner, and then set about explaining who she was to his housekeeper and butler.

"I shall need a maid and companion for the future duchess," his Grace informed his staff.

"Oh, but I don't need—"

The raised brow stopped the flow of Sadie's words. She stared him full in the face and then dropped her eyes. She was so perfect for him. He loved her sass before she submitted.

After giving a few more instructions, Richard dismissed his senior staff members and turned to Sadie. "Rule one, do not contradict me in front of staff or visitors."

"Yes, milord, I am sorry to have forgotten my place."

Richard released a sound of frustration. "Sadie, you may sass, argue, demand, disagree, and any other counteraction you wish to employ when we are alone or with close friends and family, but never in front of the servants or guests. I hold as close family, my mother and sister. Close friends are the men you met today and their wives. There are a few others but when you meet them, I will identify them as such. Have I made myself understood?"

"Yes, Richard but what if I cannot agree?"

"If important, I shall always consult you in private. If you believe I do not have the right of it, then you will request a moment."

"In front of a guest?"

"Yes, I can see what you mean. If it is something you need to tell me and you believe I will continue before you have time to have a quiet word, then we should have a signal between us so that I know you need to speak to me."

Sadie's eyes lit up. "You mean like a secret code?"

He smiled at her enthusiasm. She was going to keep him on his toes and entertained. "If you like, although I was thinking more of a touch of your ear when you have my attention."

"Oh, I do like that."

"After we are married, we will speak again about signals and codewords."

"Shall we? How exciting. You are rather more than I knew, Your Grace."

"Indeed. And you are more enchanting than I dared hope, my dear." He kissed her cheek and Sadie placed her hand over the place his lips touched.

"I'm not sure that is seemly." She blushed. "But I enjoyed it."

"We are to be married, Sarah. Would you marry with no knowledge?"

"Am I to have knowledge, sir? I don't believe I should."

"Not carnal my dear, but you should get a taste to whet your appetite. We will announce our engagement tonight, unofficially, and officially after Mother and my sister Julia arrives. Now, time to dress. Mrs. Carrier should have your room made up and a maid at your disposal."

Chapter 14 Time For Duchess Lessons

Sadie was feeling a little raw and vulnerable. Having a maid assigned to her to help, even if just for tonight, was a relief because she just didn't think she would feel confident enough to do all the dressing and preparing alone. She had missed being in a home that was alive with activity. Another woman's opinion was always preferable. However, Sadie soon learned that while another woman's help would be welcomed, she did not receive Quillie's with the same enthusiasm. Quillie appeared around Sadie's age, and she treated Sadie with unconcealed hostility.

"Am I taking you from your dinner or your betrothed or something equally vexing?"

The maid, Quillie, shook her head and seemed confused. "No milady."

Sadie wanted to correct Quillie, but she was unsure whether Richard would want her to or leave as is. She decided to address it. If the duke thought it was an error, she was sure he would have no issue with pointing it out.

"I'm not a titled lady, so calling me Miss would be perfectly appropriate and preferred."

Cranky and hungry again, the tea not sustaining her as long as she had hoped, Sadie tried to keep her tone congenial even though the woman was sending her waves of resentment. They had just met. She couldn't have done something to bother her already.

As the young woman finished buttoning her gown, a pretty periwinkle that Sadie thought brought up the color in her cheeks and the sparkle in her blue eyes, she clicked her tongue.

"It's a real pity that you have such sallow skin. The color would be lovely on a more peaches and cream complexion."

Again, the doubts of her ability to pull this duchess thing off assailed her. She held her tears and stiffened her spine, but her heart was breaking. Was life always going to bear the type of kindness brought on by sympathy? The more persistent thoughts took over, thoughts she had hoped she'd squelched.

You are surrounded by beauty. if you would only meet the standard, you could be attractive, too. Sadie almost sent the maid out immediately; however, she didn't know that much about dressing hair so she allowed her wits and strength of character to carry her through. And she could hear Lady Clarise saying in her head, "You are the lady, you are paying wages, expect good service."

"The duke is anxious to see how this looks on me. I was particularly hoping it would look as good on as when he chose it for me. He expressed the abilities of Mrs. Carrier to pick out the right person to be my maid, and so I am sure he would be disappointed in the poor woman if her choice did not prove adequate."

Without a word, Quillie dressed her hair with a simple but elegant braided twist. Sadie smiled at her ingenuity in turning things around to get the outcome she had wanted. Then Quillie made the unfortunate mistake of speaking again.

"I don't know why you care what you look like. You are not going to turn the head of a duke. You have no station in life. You are no better than me." Sadie turned to her in surprise. "Oh, aye, I know you were the sweet bit on the side for Lord Henderson after his dear wife passed. We all know. You won't be worth the dress you stand in soon. Not once the word gets out. No, you will be putting your hand out for coin and begging for mercy."

Sadie didn't know what came over her, but her moment of victory was in ashes and her tears rushed down her cheeks. Her hand raised and through the blurry haze, she delivered a resounding slap.

The room seemed to stand still and silent as a tomb as Richard fully entered the bedchamber. Sadie's hands over her face and the maid's hand over the reddening mark on her cheek, a look of hatred in her eyes. First things first.

"I do not recall your name." Richard's cold voice was not to be confused with a congenial master.

"Quillie, Your Grace."

The girl's voice was hesitant and shaky but not without a confident certainty that she was not found wanting in the situation. Neither woman knew that he had entered the scene in progress, but it was soon enough to believe punishment would be meted out and neither would come away unscathed. He wanted to end the association with this Quillie immediately, but his Darling Duchess needed to practice restraint.

"Ah, yes, Quillie. You may report to Mrs. Carrier until I come to discuss this incident with her. And Quillie?"

"Yes, sir?"

"Do not disclose any of this occurrence until I am there to take part in that conversation. Gossip is something I will not tolerate. And you would mind well my words if you do not wish to find yourself out on the street corner before the end of this very night."

Quillie's voice, which had been confidently indignant was immediately contrite and submissive. "Yes, Your Grace. Sorry, Your Grace."

Richard grunted as the maid rushed out. He cared not for her feelings at the moment. He had long forgotten the stories his friends had told of settling into their husbandly duties. Richard was so angry he needed to pull in his heightened emotions and speaking coldly to the young lady that looked to be his Sadie's age was enough to make him breathe slow and deep.

Yes, wrapping his girl in cotton wool was the best bet to keep her safe from dangers and pain outside and inside her home, but it was impractical. The very independence he loved in Sadie was the same independence that exposed her to hurts and kept him from over-coddling her, but it still ignited his need to protect. *Mine.*

"I-I am sorry, sir. I should have held my temper better, but she said horrid things that I would never expect anyone to say to me or to anyone. It implied such vulgarity between Lord Henderson and me. He doesn't deserve that for being so kind to me."

A new round of tears descended, and Richard didn't know what to do with a crying Sadie. Sassy, yes. Angry, demanding he understand her, yes, but he could not find a confident response to her pain bathed in tears. He was feeling his ire again likely because her tears made him feel inadequate to her needs. They had a dinner engagement, and it was time to address this and put a stop to her feelings of hurt and defeat and his of impotence.

"Sarah, that is quite enough."

His voice was stern. His tone left no room for negotiation. In some ways, it was a relief to take charge, and in other ways, he cringed at the response to her pain.

She nodded and attempted to rein in the overflowing fountain of tears. "I'm trying, sir."

"We have a dinner invitation that I have accepted, and it is too late to withdraw, therefore you will stop the drama and wash your face. I fear any face powder or rouge you may have used is long gone and we have no time for reapplication. Papa likes you as you are if the truth be told."

"I'm sorry, Richard. Please forgive me. I should not have risen to her taunts and lies but I simply did not have the restraint in me tonight. I will try harder, sir." She lifted sad eyes to him. "Unless you cannot tolerate it and I will understand. Shall I go home?"

Richard sighed. He would need to reassure her often while also teaching her that she was to do as her papa required. A delicate balance, to be the wife of a duke, have funds of her own, long for security and love, but not think she deserved it. He was to be her papa in one situation and her husband in another and her duke in a third. Hell, he was overwhelmed at the work that was needed between now and their nuptials.

"We have much work to do between now and when you become my duchess, but you are already my little one. I love you, Sarah, with all that I am. It is confusing, I know, but we will untangle the strands, so they weave into the pattern we choose. Yes?"

She nodded, then, as though she remembered he wanted to hear her words, "Yes, sir."

"Excellent. Now, I think it would help if we established a few rules."

"Oh, sir, more rules?"

He felt his lip tip up at the corners, but he refused to fully smile. "Now my girl, watch your tongue." He tapped her nose to soften his words. "None of that sassing you love to engage in. We will discuss the lack of decorum later, but for now, if I call you Sadie, you are speaking to your papa. If I call you Sarah, you are speaking to the duke and later, your husband. Will that help in understanding what it is that I need from you? What you can expect from me?"

"Possibly? But at least when you call me Sarah, I know I must be on my best behavior and if I am Sadie, I may be sassy."

"With consequences of course, but yes. Papa disciplines with his hand and sometimes his leather so I would be very careful how you respond to him."

She nodded somberly. "Yes, I will, sir."

"Good. Now, that was Sadie who slapped her maid, so it is Sadie who is getting spanked."

"But I didn't do it. I mean, I did slap her, but she was so horrible to me. She deserved it."

"Sadie, being justified doesn't mean your actions are right. You may send her from the room or leave the room yourself. You may never slap or push or any other manner of rude response. Do I make myself clear? If it is very difficult, go to your papa or find Mrs. Carrier."

"Yes, sir, but I don't want to be spanked. I have learned my lesson."

"I am reinforcing it." He reached for her and quickly leaned her against the edge of her bed.

"Papa, my hair."

"Is well pinned I expect. Hold on to it if you are concerned, but I will not let you get away with that type of behavior without addressing it, hair be damned."

"Oh, Papa, you have a naughty mouth. Can I punish you?" She heard her voice change its quality but was too caught up in the present situation to pay it much mind.

"No, but you will get one less swat as my penance."

"I'm not sure that is quite right," Sadie replied with suspicion.

"It is because I wanted to feel my hand on your backside all ten times. Now I only get nine."

She giggled. "Silly papa."

"Indeed." The next minute was filled with her squeals and begging for him to stop.

"I'm such a bad choice for you." Another substantial swat landed in the center of her backside, and Sadie screeched. "You already reached nine, sir."

"So, I did, but this was for believing that you were not good enough for me. We are good enough for each other and I will not hear those words from you again."

He sat her up and helped his Darling put herself to rights. "But you expected, your *family* expects, so much more."

"They require that I be happy and that is happening right now. We are happy or we will be once all the work is done. When I say that I will love, honor, and protect you, we shall be ready to begin that chapter of our lives. Until then, we are preparing and what you and I envision for our life is all that is important."

"But surely your mother wants you to marry well."

The duke grumbled. "I am marrying well. I am to be your husband, which is to be envied by all other, unattached men. Now, go wash your face, little one and we will pray that your skin clears before we arrive at Thayer's, otherwise they will know you have been naughty."

"Or you have been a beast."

"Very possibly."

"Are you sure you want me with you?"

"Very. Now I must go take care of a naughty maid. You have ten minutes to repair your face and be in the entry, ready to leave." He kissed her lightly. "And no rubbing your derriere."

"Of course, not... Richard." He turned to look at Sadie. "Do you intend to chastise her as well?"

"Oh, my dear, I reserve my hand touching a woman's backside to my woman's backside."

She sniffed. "That is only as it should be."

Her pert answer did make him smile. Her spirit was strong. He knew she would soothe her sit-upon the moment he left her, but Richard was more than satisfied that they had made inroads to establishing the distinctions between Papa and Richard, Sadie and Sarah, and his expectations for his duchess.

Sitting in the carriage, Richard was glad to see that whatever Sarah had done, she had successfully repaired her red eyes and face. It was still pink but with her periwinkle dress, it complimented her.

"You look beautiful in that gown, my dear. It is incredibly sweet, and yet sophisticated."

"Thank you, sir." She said nothing else, and Richard fell into contemplation.

Sadie was very subdued since leaving the house and Richard wanted to make sure she was recovered but didn't want to return to the distasteful incident. Her pride needed to heal, so he said nothing in the hopes that the ladies would buoy her up.

He hadn't said anything about the maid's discipline either but after talking to Mrs. Carrier, he decided to leave that to her. Mr. Carrier tended to pull out his strap, but Mrs. Carrier tended to assign more chores. That was something he needed to begin expanding, his discipline methods. It was important now and he didn't want spanking to be associated with wrongdoings only, but with pleasure at times.

Sadie was cute as she tried to find a way to sit on her punished bottom. He had to bite his tongue to stop from grinning. Lesson received then.

"Sadie, stop moving around. Do you need to use the necessity?"

Her gasp of outrage was comical. It was easy to get a response from his Darling.

"I am not a child that you would ask such a question."

"For Sarah, I would agree, but I must think it is Sadie who is having trouble finding a comfortable seat and I would ask her such a thing. If you would just sit lightly, it would be better. I shall have to place a pillow in the carriage for my naughty girl."

"No, I like the... yes, that would be kind of you."

Her face went white in discovery and now was blood red in her realization. Richard looked out the window so his grin would not give him away. She was aroused sitting on her chastisement. Excellent. That was better than he had hoped for so soon.

Richard and Sarah were the last ones to arrive. "Apologies, we had some last-minute details that we had to address, and it took longer than expected."

Richard explained their delay and continued to another subject without even a pause. Sarah was finding it a little more difficult to do so. She had only met the men today and their wives, never. The Laird took the lead as they were in his home.

"Lady Morgan, please sit where you are comfortable, and I will make the introductions. To remind you, I am the Laird, everyone calls me such, and my wife Cairistine. This is Lord Thayer, and his wife Annalise." Sarah nodded and continue to acknowledge with kind words after each introduction.

The Laird continued. "This gentleman, as you may remember, is Lord Kendrick, and his lovely wife, Genevieve. Lord Ashton and his wife, Rosemary who is also my cousin. Then we have My Lord Duke Trenton and his lovely wife, Sofia. And finally, we have My Lord Duke Jasper who has yet to find a companion who will take him as her spouse." Jasper shook his head but smiled and everyone else seemed to enjoy the joke. "He has, however, found a lovely creature, Lady Evangelina Montague with which to share the evening."

That good woman smiled and seemed not at all put out at the introduction. "Please call me Eve if Evangelina is too much. I am quite content with that fact."

"I totally understand as I am usually known as Cairis for my name is quite unique to Londoners. My husband is our resident Scot, better known as the Black Laird, but don't let that name fool you, he is as gentle as a lamb."

Richard laughed. "A hungry one."

Dinner was announced soon afterward, and the meal seemed to go on forever. Sarah enjoyed the women's hint of playfulness with their husbands and amongst themselves. Richard sat on her right and continued to help her throughout the meal. He had her wine glass refilled, but much to her chagrin, stopped it from being refilled a third time. He cut her meat, and quietly demanded more bites before she could survey desserts.

Fortunately, when Sarah slid her gaze around the table, she saw her fellow females were experiencing the same treatment from their husbands. They saw nothing wrong with their husbands cutting their meat, directing their attention to one bit of food or another, and Cairistine's husband, the Laird, even moved her wine glass in front of his plate and she was left with milk or tea. She was not happy. Evidently, the Laird wasn't concerned.

Even Lord Jasper seemed to naturally take on the care of his companion who hesitated once or twice but soon seemed content in the behaviors.

Otherwise, the group was jovial and well informed she realized as she listened to their conversations. The women as well as the men. It was also obvious that these men, unlike most of society as she was allowed to observe, were much like Lord Henderson. Their marriages appeared to be similar to her late benefactors. They were like what she imagined Richard expected their marriage to be. Sarah resolved to discuss things with these wives before she signed the book and was wed.

Leaning over near the end of the meal, Richard whispered in Sarah's ear, "Are you well? You have gone very quiet."

"I am well, sir, but I fear I have used the wrong utensil for the last course."

"Oh, yes? Never fear. I have the solution."

He patted her hand, but he looked pointedly at her lips, and she did not have to guess his thoughts. He wanted to kiss her. Sadie glanced down and saw his manhood and it appeared to have difficulty staying hidden. She wasn't sure if she should be shocked or embarrassed. She'd seen male appendages on children but never a man and the thought left her with a reaction she was unprepared to have. The heat rose up her neck and into her face.

He leaned down again and whispered. "You are not allowed to look at my anatomy in that way. It will make it impossible for me to leave the table. I am having difficulty keeping things under control as it is."

His tone was severe, but it only made Sarah want to giggle. Mmm, power in their marriage was suddenly a dual event. It was delicious. She looked away and spoke to Rosemary who was seated at her left.

Dessert was not a fiasco because Richard came to her rescue. She watched him touch the sticky toffee pudding to his lips with his spoon and fed it to her. He left her with his spoon, and then he took her spoon and used it for his dessert, and no one was the wiser. She fell a little more in love with him that night.

The gentlemen went to the library to partake of their after-dinner liquors, and she followed the women into the roomy parlor. While Cairis offered to bring out the cards or other entertainment, these women had suddenly gone from very proper women with exquisite manners to close friends chatting freely. Then Cairis offered sherry, or another glass of wine. Sadie hesitated.

"I'm not sure Rich-, um, the duke would be happy with me choosing to have more drink. I should wait and ask him."

Cairistine shook her head, moving her luscious red hair. "Well, that won't do, because if you ask, he will say no and we are all likely to get the official frown, even though they do not actually care."

Rosemary nodded. "She is right, I'm afraid."

Cairistine spoke again. "We aren't alone, our male protectors are with us. Listen, your duke well knows that we have this after dinner. It's likely why he stopped you at the table. So you could have another here." She poured her own sherry, and the others took their glasses.

Genevieve didn't contribute to the conversation, but she did take her glass and sip the liquor.

Sofia smiled and said, "Besides, it tastes sweeter if you don't talk about it. Our men, they're possessive and—"

"And protective," added Rosemary.

"And domineering," said Cairistine.

"Are you not distressed by the overly close attention they spend observing and interfering with you?" asked Eve.

Cairis shook her head. "Not in the slightest. It can be annoying at times, but you never worry if anyone will notice you in a room, for he always does. It is exciting and if he catches you when you do not wish him to, it can be titillating."

Annalise smiled and touched Sadie's hand. "And we love them completely." The others murmured agreement.

Genevieve finally spoke. "Now, tell us all about yourself and how you found the duke. We are curious and the sooner you tell us, the sooner we will leave you alone and move to less invasive subjects."

"Oh, I'm not sure if I should say anything."

Sofia settled into her chair. "You are joining our lady's group which includes all of us and Julia, Griffin's sister, on occasion."

Sadie listened to more banter, and she slowly eased into the bits of the story she felt comfortable sharing. It appeared to meet the ladies' need for information because they all made satisfied murmurs and went on to more diverse subjects.

"When are you to marry?" asked Rosemary. "We can come to your breakfast since you have no relatives."

"That would be so kind, however, I'm not sure of anything."

The room was quiet. "Did he ask you?" inquired Cairis.

"More like he informed me."

The women nodded. Genevieve asked, "Are you to have the banns read?"

"Yes. The first one this Sunday in his country chapel and one here at Saint George's Hanover Square I suppose, but Richard, um, the duke is taking care of that."

"When we are alone with only each other and no other person, it is perfectly acceptable for us to call our husbands by their given names. Except for the Laird. I believe he is called that in all circumstances but the most formal," said Annalise. Cairis nodded her agreement.

Sadie smiled because she had stumbled over what to call him in their company all evening. "The problem is he is not a lord, not a proper one, but saying Your Grace or the duke is so formal."

Sofia nodded. "It might get doors opened, but it leads to many awkward conversations. I try to avoid awkward at all costs."

Tea was brought in, and Annalise quickly sent the evidence of sherry out with the maid. "We don't want to make things difficult, do we?" She shrugged as it if were a necessary evil and assisted Cairis as she poured tea.

The men entered the room moments later. Conversation continued until Sadie felt completely exhausted. Richard noticed and began their goodbyes.

"Were you not staying the night?" asked the Laird.

"My townhouse is quite comfortable. I have impressive help and they have worked hard to make it ready for us but accept my thanks for the offer."

"Ach, aye."

By the time they were home and Sadie tucked into bed, it was very late, nearly two in the morning, and she was asleep the moment her head hit her pillow.

Chapter 15 Time To Take Charge

Sadie was sure that she was in the presence of the Duke of Amesbury all morning. He was very opinionated and occasionally seemed to force himself to slow down and explain things to Sadie.

"Sadie, papa is trying to work on this ledger. Maybe a walk in the garden would entertain you."

"Are you saying that because you want me to leave you alone to think? Are you treating me like a child because you believe I don't have the intelligence to understand this ledger, or because you have taken over and believe me a nuisance? Or was that your plan all along?"

Richard had laid down his pencil and leaned back in Lord Henderson's chair. The one he used at his desk when he was settling accounts and meeting with staff. Richard had said they would address staff tomorrow once he had a handle on what was needed. He brought some of his own work with him to make sure he didn't miss his own appointments.

Sadie had enjoyed learning about all the accounts at the elbow of her benefactor and later, when he died, she had perused them all carefully. She hadn't revealed the other set of books to Richard all morning and now she applauded her foresight.

"I'm sorry, love. It is a set of books I don't know and am trying to familiarize myself with them. They are rather scant, but straightforward. I should have a good grasp after this afternoon. Can you ask your maid for tea please?"

Sadie sat hard in the chair across the desk from Richard and scowled. "I don't know why I must have this maid."

"It is a learning experience. We have already discussed this."

"But I don't understand why I should be punished to suffer through Quillie's discipline."

"It is a life lesson to learn to tolerate the intolerable. It is also good to practice for when you are my duchess."

"You are being unfair, and it is unnecessary. I curbed my tongue as long as I could and endured chastising when I lost the battle. To suffer another penalty is inexcusable. It's cruel. If you want tea, then I shall make it. I know how."

"I do not doubt you know how to make tea, but your tone is bordering on disrespect. I have decided you need to learn to work well with Quillie as she is representative of all the staff you will control as the duchess. Quillie must learn her place as a maid employed by us."

She tried a different tack. "I know all about those accounts as his lordship showed me and I know all about making tea because the cook showed me. I also know about not allowing staff to dominate you and when they have stepped out of line, for I have been privy to both. Lady Henderson taught me well. If you choose to disrespect me by ignoring my intelligence and talents, then you are a lesser man than I had thought. I'm not sure we will suit after all."

Sadie left the room and nearly had an attack of the vapors, something she would never ascribe to, but her heart was pounding so vigorously. Her body seemed to float in a whirlwind of movement. She was nauseous. She placed her hand on her chest and tried to concentrate on breathing. It was a very difficult task. Her head was pounding in time with her heart. She hardly took notice of the office door opening until she inhaled his familiar scent.

Sadie looked into Richard's confused eyes as they settled on her leaning against the wall panel next to the door. He reached for her.

"Sadie, princess, what is wrong?"

She couldn't speak, couldn't put into words an answer because her mind couldn't formulate one. She simply stared at him in distress. Her vision was spotty now.

"Bloody hell."

He lifted her from her position against the wall and all she could do was lay in his arms as he carried her into the library next door to the study.

"Hold on, love."

He left from her view and shouted with a mighty command in his voice. "Quillie, bring me a wet cloth."

"I am well, sir. I just needed to have a moment."

Richard pushed for an answer. "What happened? You are white as a ghost and you *were* sick, I could tell."

"What happened, sir? Oh, Miss, are you well?"

Richard placed the cloth on her forehead. When Sadie tried to move it, he made a deep throaty rumble that sounded his irritation. She dropped her hand.

"Yes, I'll be fine, both of you. I just need to sit up and settle myself. I was dizzy... I was hot and my heart was pounding and... it was nothing. If you had not come out of the study so quickly, sir, I would have recovered, and you would have been none the wiser."

"You would have told me."

"Of course not, sir. Why would I have told you if there was nothing to tell?"

Richard started to say something and then checked himself before turning to Quillie and saying, "I want you to go make tea."

"Oh, but sir... yes, Your Grace, sorry, Your Grace." Quillie curtsied and then rushed off to do his bidding.

"Richard, you scared her."

"Oh, yes? The way I see it, she could do with a little fright, the cheeky thing. I don't allow too much familiarity with anyone, but especially not my staff."

"And yet, you would have me keep her."

"Yes, because you can be rather cheeky yourself. I like you that way. I do not enjoy Quillie taking on that behavior."

Sadie sat up and nodded. "Papa, I think I was angry at you."

"Yes, I'm sure you were but when, specifically, are we speaking of?"

"When you dismissed me earlier." Richard nodded but said nothing. "You can't treat me as though I am a child when I am a fully grown adult. It is demeaning."

"This is a learning experience for both of us. I am a man with high expectations and often dismiss the women in my life, Julia and my mother, mainly because they do not care to be involved in the estate's running or the business affairs elsewhere. They take care of tending to the needs of the tenants on the estate when appropriate, but all transactions are mine to handle."

"But I don't want to be pushed to the side, sir. I am happy being caretaker of the tenants and the household's daily needs, but I also have a head for figures and problem-solving that I cannot, now that I have learned, hide away."

Richard leaned over and placed a kiss on her lips. "You are right, my dear. I am going to have to make adjustments in the way I perform my duties as well as you. But you may not become so angry that you have another episode like the one you just experienced. I cannot spend my days worrying about that outcome."

"Yes, Richard."

"And I do not give you permission to become that angry again."

"I shall try, but if that is the case, sir, then you must listen to me and not discard my words out of hand."

Richard pulled her into his arms and Sadie cuddled into his embrace. "I will do my best. And the next time you leave me so angry you bring on an episode, I shall nurse you back to health and then turn you over my knee."

Sadie grinned. "Yes, sir."

Quillie returned with the tea and cuddle time was over. Richard was oversolicitous until she huffed her exasperation.

"Understood, my dear. I must get back to the accounts. Come when you are ready and we will examine them together."

"I have something I should do first, Your Grace. I'll be along directly."

He hesitated, possibly debating what she was about but decided to not pursue his thoughts and returned to the study. Sarah thought she should do as Richard had said and establish ground rules for her staff. She thought her role was to be more personable with them, but still show her position. Now was the time to put that plan into action.

Quillie returned and paused at the door before entering when she saw there was only Sarah.

"Quillie, sit and let us discuss the situation."

"Miss?"

"The situation of you being my maid. I am not happy about it as I am sure, deep down, you are not as well. However, the duke says I must keep you for the time being and I have decided to make the most of it. I require help to dress when I go out or when we are entertaining, as well as my hair coiffured. I require my clothes kept clean and wrinkle-free as much as possible. I also require you to make sure that you lay my night clothes out on my bed and my fire lit when the chill greets us in the morning."

"Yes, Miss."

Sadie nodded. "Otherwise, as things come up, I will ask. Sometimes there are requirements I don't know about until I am told and then I will inform you. We must employ the best methods to get along and you are required to fully participate. I am let to understand that if I or the duke believes you are not putting forth your best effort, you will find yourself without employment and I don't wish that on you."

"No. Thank you, Miss."

There seemed to be some apprehension on Quillie's face and Sadie could remember that feeling only too well. Her heart seemed to soften, but she bolstered herself. These things needed to be said.

"Finally, I was Lady Henderson's companion and then Lord Henderson's after she had gone. I have never been more than a companion, but they were my benefactors when my mother passed when I was eleven. My mother had been their housekeeper and since my lord and lady could not have children, they became surrogates for me. I was lucky. The duke and Lord Henderson were acquainted and so the introductions were made. I will be married to the Duke of Amesbury because he wills it and I accept that sentiment. That is a non-changing fact. Either you accept that or pack up now for I won't tolerate the way you have treated me or spoken to me again. His Grace will be even less tolerant. Am I understood?"

"Yes, Miss."

"Good. Now, let's put all of this away from us and be more pleasant. I recommend being ready to leave at a moment's notice for I have learned that His Grace doesn't tend to exhibit much patience at times." Sadie smiled and shrugged. "And yet, sometimes his forbearance is unsurpassed."

"I'll be ready, Miss."

"Good."

Sadie rose and walked out of the room in her Sarah persona and was rather proud of the headway she had made with Quillie. It was too bad that she couldn't have her as a friend. Sarah walked into the study with the weight of not having any real friends heavy on her mind. Yes, she had met the women of Richard's friends and they were very nice, but all were polished and refined, and while welcoming enough, simply not the people she would have known how to be friends with.

"Sarah? Why the long face? What has saddened you? I have said we can work on the accounts together and other things."

Sarah looked up and shook her head, offering a tentative smile. "I'm just lonely for my old life. I will get past it, but it was familiar, and since I have no family—"

"Yet. I am your family now and soon it will be official. I have a mother and sister who will be happy for another woman to join their inner circle."

"I suppose, but it's still new and unfamiliar, isn't it? Your mother may not like me, and your sister might believe I am all wrong for you and she wouldn't be in error."

"Do I have such poor judgment?"

"What? No, it's just, well, in this case, it does look like it."

"You have been told that I am known as the Daring Duke. Even before I was the title holder, I had well established my penchant to take risks no one else would take and they turn out profitable. I have good judgment. I am no fool."

"How can you be so sure about us?"

"Because, in business, I can be rather ruthless about my choices, several of which seem too farfetched or risky to entertain, and yet, I am drawn to make the deal. Without exception, I have not regretted those challenging choices, but most times I am told it would be a daring move and later how insightful I am. So being daring has filled my coffers, made me more open to risks and possibilities, and I am extending my territory. Where others see folly, I see great probability."

"So, I am a folly you want to prove to others you can make good? I don't know if I can be that experimental project for you."

Richard ran his hand through his hair making his usually impeccable style, less so. She wanted to smooth it for him. Could it work? Did she want to be that person for him? She knew how unlikely the coupling would be in society. She questioned him and he was confident, but why? What did he see that she or others could not?

Her mind wandered to the women she had met last week. They were to all come for dinner tomorrow evening at Richard's home. She thought of the clerk he had hired to take an inventory of the valuables, catalog each room of all its pertinent contents, and the books he was intent on unraveling. She knew why Richard was successful in things he wanted; he invested his time and considerable energy into the task. He ensured it thrived because he didn't allow the venture to do anything else.

Was their union the same? Would he put in the time, energy, and genuine effort in the marriage to make sure it not only survived but thrived? How could he do that when he had never been married before? How could she?

"What are you thinking, Sarah?" The closeness of Richard's voice startled her, but his calming hand on her shoulder relaxed her.

"That I wish I had your confidence this was going to work. Truth be told, I don't even know how to begin being married to you. Your status alone is more than I can wrap my head around."

"I am just a man, my dear. Flesh and blood with feelings and opinions, just like every other man. It's just that this man wants you, and that confuses you. You wonder, why you? And possibly the responsibility of that position scares you a bit."

She nodded, and he led her to the only place to sit, outside of the desk chairs. Once seated on the two-person settee, he turned toward Sarah. She melted at the raw emotion on his face.

"I love you. I know it isn't the manly thing to do; tell the woman he is going to marry that he has more than affection towards her, but I am in love with you, Sarah. I don't always show it, nor do I always exhibit the mannerisms of a man in love, but take my word that it is a truth."

"How can you say that, when we have not seen each other for such a long time?"

"I can because I began to fall in love with you that first night we met. I didn't know it at the time, but it is nonetheless true. You accepted that I caught you spying, and were submissive and yet showed your sassiness in sparring with your words."

"It was shameful."

Richard chuckled. "You were the first to pull me from my serious-minded endeavors. Since I had to take over the estates, even while my father was alive, it was sobering for a man of my young age. Since that time, I have done well. I do not deny it, but it came at a cost. I expected that I could only do one thing well. When I met you, I thought that the cost might not have been so exorbitant as I had feared. That I could have a wife I adored, a family I was proud of, and continue being prosperous in my business dealings."

"Indeed, it does sound risky."

"Very risky. You were a breath of fresh air. You still are. I had tried to put you in the background of my life, and it worked for a while. It worked until you lost Lady Henderson, then I gave marriage some thought again. That is when I reached out to Henderson. He was less than enthusiastic that I might marry you before you were ready."

"I would have done whatever he told me to do."

"And that is why he left you independent. He didn't want you to do what others told you to do. Concerning your future happiness, he didn't want to be that person, either. It took a while to come to that conclusion, but I see it now. It's why he gave a letter to the solicitor. He wrote it, ready to post when he had passed."

"But if I have free will and this autonomy is so wonderful, then why don't I feel overjoyed at the situation he was so gracious to provide for me?"

"I believe there are several things at play here. You belong here, in this house, with the same people you always had in your life."

"Yes, that is what I said earlier, the familiarity. Only it hasn't worked out that way."

"Right, and the next thing is that change is something you have rarely had to endure. You haven't moved, you haven't had to do anything different or challenging."

"No, that isn't true. I lost people. And I had to endure Lady Henderson's training."

"And Lord Henderson's."

"Yes. And I had to follow the house rules and theirs. They rather restricted me on what I could do, know, and experience. I later wondered if they thought they could keep me with them forever."

"Yes, I saw that, but the outcome is that you are the perfect Darling for me. You want me to do for you, plan, execute that plan, and take that burden off you when you feel the need to be coddled. I want that innocent connection, that devotion and sassiness that you bring to our relationship. When you want to let go of the reins, I take them. When you reach for them again, in nearly all cases, except discipline, I will release them back to you."

Richard had pulled Sadie into his lap. "But when your mother and sister come, they will not want me as you do. They will see the impropriety of me wedding you, and you will bow to their pressure."

"I run my home and myself, my sister until she is married is under my protection and rule, and my mother will concede to my wishes."

"Richard, would it be an awful waste of money if I were to have some vetted staff here? I think I would like to stay here until we wed. Just in case."

"It isn't required and is unnecessary."

"Possibly, possibly not, but I still would like to be in my environment until then. Please, papa?"

Richard grinned and pinched her thigh. Sadie yelped. "You are mixing the personas, and it is clever. Papa says he doesn't want you to be under another roof but mine. The duke says he understands the benefit for you and to ward off gossipmongers. Quillie will stay with you. I'll send another staff member while Mrs. Carrier and I pick your staff."

"With me. We must interview here, but you may pick the candidates."

He laughed again. "You are coming into the duchess mindset, but I warn you to be careful of your boundaries. Right, you may interview with us, but we make no decisions in front of the applicant. We wait until the person is out of the room, and at the end of the interviews, we will decide and share our decisions. The hope is that within 24 hours of acceptance, the staff member will be in service."

She nodded. "Yes, that would be acceptable. Thank you."

He raised his eyebrow to comment, but he must have changed his mind, for he simply nodded agreement. After some discussion, Sadie brought out the authentic ledgers. The ones with intricate detail.

"Where were these?" Richard asked as he opened and perused the pages.

"I had them hidden, as Lord Henderson instructed me to do upon his death."

"What else do you have hidden away?"

"Well, I gave most of my funds to Mr. Shackleford to hold so the Flanders didn't steal it all from me when I slipped out of the house. I have detailed records. Other than that, some coin, some jewelry of Lady Henderson, and some paperwork of ownership of this house and the contents inside. A bill of sale. His letter to me. My notes of what I am to do after his death, not much else."

Richard sat for a few moments, examining the ledgers in front of him. "Can you show me?"

"The places where I hid things?"

"If you wouldn't mind." Sadie fidgeted and didn't respond. "Sadie, what is troubling you?"

"I'm having difficulty showing anyone the hiding spots. It's my security, and I'm too recently violated in that way to be easily forthcoming. It isn't you, I promise, but..." she shrugged.

When Richard responded, his tone was gentle. "I can understand that, and so when you are ready to trust me completely, then you will show me. Until then, I will wait."

Sadie brightened. "You will?"

"I will."

AS RICHARD, SADIE, and the clerk sifted through the inventory, entering each room in Sadie's house methodically, they added staff that included Quillie. That young lady seemed to draw protectively over her mistress after hearing more of the story of what had happened to her from the new housekeeper, Mrs. Arnold. That woman set Quillie straight on her new mistress. She seemed to take the girl under her wing, which was helpful for everyone.

Richard had worked his magic and enticed Mr. and Mrs. Arnold back with slightly more pay and the run of the household again. The new employers had offered the Arnolds an immense household to run when they left Henderson House, but it was so big that the lord, who had no lady, wanted two housekeepers. One for the downstairs and one for the upper floors. The conflicts reached a fevered pitch when the other housekeeper was seen and heard spending too much time in the lord's bedchamber.

Sadie was happy having her home bustling with activity and direction. She officially stayed in the house, but Richard would come and stay until late, only to arrive in the morning again to have breakfast. As they worked, they discussed what to do with the house after they were married.

"We could rent it during the off-season and during the season we are here, we could be in residence. Then I wouldn't rent, and you could easily keep the home well lived in." Sarah nodded. "Yes, homes should be lived in, or they would become simply a house. But what of the Arnolds? They can't find other employment every year."

"No, Mother has always said that after I am married, she is not the type of mother-in-law that would be comfortable in the same home. Two mistresses are never good. My paternal grandmother stayed for a short time before going to be with her sister. Mother does not want to repeat that experience. She would like to have the dowager house, and she can keep her housekeeper and butler, her companion, and the maid. She may even take the cook if she so desires."

"Then the Arnolds would come with us? Oh, Richard, I would like that immensely."

"Good, there is that business done, then. Now Mother and Julia will be here any day. I would like you to come and meet them when they arrive."

"Shouldn't you discuss things with them first? I mean... they might not wish to meet me."

Richard smiled. "They will be delighted. Besides, they have no choice in who I decide will be my Darling Duchess. They are intelligent, reasonable women who want me happy."

"If you say so, Your Grace."

"Saucy minx."

Chapter 16 Time For Alliances

Every six months, Richard would rent a residence while in London, as most of his acquaintances did, because they had estates that needed their attention during the rest of the year. Some, like Lord Jasper, preferred to live in London for most of the year, as his parents and younger siblings still resided on the family estate. Jasper, as was highly uncommon, was born a duke. Richard's business and estate were all on his shoulders, so spending a year in either locale was impossible.

Lord Dwyer had passed away recently, which is why the home, which had been a full-time residence prior to Richard renting it, was available at all. He was considering purchasing it as the heirs had approached him. He would have to discuss this with Sarah. It was an odd feeling to have someone to discuss things with that would see them as he did, for the good they would do for the family.

Purchasing property was what Richard did, and he wasn't sure Sarah was interested in more than Henderson House. Finding that fine line between sharing the family estate's business and over-involving his wife would take some finesse. His first goal was to keep her happy. The rest would follow as it did.

Richard already had a list of the items he wanted to be removed from Henderson House and taken back to Amesbury House for Sarah, but he hadn't discussed this with her yet. She was so overwhelmed since his mother and Julia arrived yesterday, that he thought he'd present her with the list after the nuptials. Yes, it was cowardly in that he didn't want to upset the delicate balance they had, but he also did not want to stress her any further.

Richard finished his breakfast as he contemplated what the next days would be like. He expected quite an uproar today because it was the first opportunity, they would have to address his letter to the womenfolk, which was delivered the same day his letter of the announcement was delivered to his cler-gyman.

The banns had been read in Wiltshire thrice now, and there was nothing holding them back from marriage except that the meeting had not yet taken place between the women. They had heard the banns and read the letter certi-fying the banns without protest. He awaited that letter before setting the date.

While he applauded Henderson for providing for Sadie, he didn't antici-pate the amount of property, both building and interior possessions, that he had actually left her. In addition to that, he had not expected the sum Hender-son left her in cash for her upkeep. The solicitor hesitated to return the bulk of it, and Richard understood.

Why Lord Henderson had not created a guardian in a more formal sense, he could not even fathom. The saving grace there was that he asked Richard to cover that necessity if he declined to take her to the altar himself. She had already endured what her trusting nature and naivete had provided her. He would have made the guardianship formal without pause if she hadn't agreed to be his duchess. And she would have been very upset about that outcome. The footman had just poured the duke more coffee when his sister entered the room in a sweep of bad manners.

"Richard, where is your Sarah? I thought she had no family to stay with."

Richard looked at his sister with a raised eyebrow. "If my memory serves me right, impatience is not a virtue, Julia."

"Yes, well, it is a personality flaw. Where is she?"

"Have you acquainted yourself with the new staff yet, Julia?" asked Richard.

"No, but since we brought several from Amesbury, I don't see why I should care to do that."

She filled her plate at the sideboard and sat at the table. A maid poured tea for her, and her napkin was in place before their mother came in sans her com-panion.

"Do not pester your brother. He is a busy man and will introduce us to his betrothed when he has time. I do hope it is before they recite their vows."

Richard rolled his eyes and sighed exaggeratedly. "Sarah is waiting to meet you. I usually have morning tea with her, so if you would like to go with me, I'd be happy to escort you."

"I will have only finished dressing by late morning," complained Julia.

"Stop whining, dear. It is unbecoming." Lady Margaret turned to Richard. "We will be ready by 10:30, if that will suffice."

"Perfect. Please excuse me. I have matters that need my attention."

Sarah was becoming worried about the marriage the longer he waited, so if he were to get her to the altar soon, there was work to be done. The introductions would be over today, the questions answered, and the preparations started for the breakfast afterward. He rose to leave. There was much to do.

"Oh, yes, dear, I forgot to tell you that you should have a letter on your desk in the library sent by the pastor."

"Brilliant. Thank you. I shall see you ladies soon."

Now he could start on his final arrangements. In the last two weeks, with the guidance of Mrs. Carrier, then Mrs. Arnold for Henderson House, he'd chosen good staff personally. Something he rarely did, but keeping his princess safe was imperative. Now Mrs. Carrier informed him that she and Mr. Carrier had employed three additional staff. What would they need with so many?

"There will be parties and dances to give and attend. The visitations will increase tenfold once the women are back out into society. And now that you will be married soon Your Grace, it will be all hands on deck."

"Yes, but I had thought to stay at Henderson House when we married."

"And then, they have only a few staff, so the loan of some of ours will be necessary. You've no idea the amount of work keeping a house is in the high season, sir."

"Thank you, Mrs. Carrier. You are right, of course. Tonight we will have Lady Sarah joining us for dinner. Tomorrow, you and Mrs. Arnold had better have a planning session for the engagement dinner and the wedding breakfast. I'll settle on the date after I return from the church."

Richard was impatient and after escorting his mother and his sister to Henderson House and introducing them to Sarah, he sat while his womenfolk asked questions. Sarah was answering with very deliberate responses.

"Milady, the planning committee is here," announced Quillie. "Mrs. Arnold has instructed that another tea tray be prepared."

"Lady Thayer, Lady Ashton, Lady O'Leary, Lady Kendrick, and the Duchess of Trenton."

"How did they all arrive in one carriage?" asked Julia.

"We could have done," said Lady Kendrick, "however, my husband decided he wanted to have a chat with Your Grace."

"Excellent choice. With so much company, I shall excuse myself and leave you ladies to it. Kendrick and I will commandeer one carriage, the smaller of the two, and leave you ladies to find your way home. Mother, you and Julia may do the same in our carriage. Do not stay too late, ladies. You all have a dinner to attend this evening."

"Sir," asked Quillie at the door, "Shall I have the house decline all other visitors today?"

"Yes, excellent idea."

"Your Grace, should it not be my decision?"

"I believe this is all that your ladyship can handle today. This company will spend more than a quarter hour, I believe. Better that you do not entertain more."

"Agreed. But I could if I wanted to."

Sarah's hand slid to touch her ear, and Richard held his tongue. Today was too taxing already without taking time out to exert his dominance.

"Indeed, my dear."

The recently arrived women began chatting as Richard closed the door. He dared not look into Sarah's eyes at the moment for fear she would stare him dead. She had been inundated since the week following the first banns being read. Now that Saint George's was done as well, the date could be set and the sooner the better.

It didn't sit right with Richard that he was unable to speak with Sarah alone today. It was the first time since he had declared his love for her that he had not. Something settled in him each time they spoke, and it had become his habit to arrive during breakfast, share the meal, and then oversee the house with Mr. Arnold before taking Sarah to walk in the garden or showing her the shops where she might like to commission her new clothes.

The ladies, as he called them in a group, had taken over the dressing needs and showed Sarah how to make those things her own domain. Richard was glad to leave that to the females. Now that his mother and Julia had arrived, he knew they would look to enhance their wardrobes for the season, which would begin within the month. He hoped to be leg-shackled by then to avoid any unpleasantness in that regard.

Julia was drawing the eye of young men with shocking consistency, now putting Richard in the precarious situation of guarding her. As a child, he had naturally protected her. As a young lady, it was taking on a whole new meaning. The stakes were much higher. While this should have been his father's job to watch out for her innocence, Richard knew the job and what it entailed. The duke's death did not add more to his son's duties.

What Richard did not relish was his mother looking for a suitor. But, as the dowager duchess had pointed out, if it is time to look for an appropriate gentleman for Julia, she might as well use the time to her advantage so that he didn't have to do this again. How did one guard over his mother when she was casting her net? The devil only knew. Thankfully, one woman under his care was secured or soon would be.

Richard was relieved he didn't have to enforce the letter that Henderson sent him, asking him to take guardianship over Sarah until she married. Richard was honored that Henderson trusted him, but he shuddered to think what Sarah would say if she had known. Thank goodness she would never have need of that information.

After the errand at St. George's, date in hand, Richard and Kendrick stopped at their club to have tea. He was famished, as it had been quite a time since breakfast.

"Now that you have the date, do you think your mother will be happy with your choice?"

"I've no idea, but I hope she is doing the eagle-eyed mama routine for Julia and subtly casting her own net. She will be occupied with parties and such, so I suppose Sarah and I will have to attend as well. I won't have to worry about Sarah, for this church date ensures we will have those formalities dispensed with before the first Cotillion."

"You won't need to attend all of them, surely."

"No, only the important ones. I will escort on the first and later in the season. Mama has every occasion mapped out and has informed me of each one."

Kendrick took a drink from his ale. "Unless hostesses invite Sarah, as your new duchess, to the events. Then you will be almost honor bound to attend."

"I had forgotten that they might want the new couple to attend so the gossiping old women can share with their husbands and thereby start their season's entertainment. I'm not sure how my Sarah will handle that."

"I'll check with Sofia to see that they ensured she had enough attire."

"And gloves. Sarah has the incredible knack of soiling every pair she wears."

"It comes from being your little Darling. We all know of the challenge. And slippers. They become so soiled; they cannot be cleaned. Sofia has several pairs not even fit for leaving the house."

Richard nodded. "All good information to have. I am learning."

"We are all still learning except maybe Thayer. I believe he was born old."

The men laughed in their agreement.

Richard strode into Henderson House and sent the maid in search of Sarah. He had to hold her in his arms. Touch her skin, smell her sweetness. He was eager to touch her intimately. Open the petals of her secret flower and bathe his fingers in her slippery heat. He needed to claim her, and waiting another week and a half was almost too long.

"Lady Sarah sends her regrets, Your Grace." The young maid hesitated.

Richard allowed the footman to help him with his coat, hat, and gloves. "Did she indeed."

"Yes, Your Grace. I'm so sorry."

"Go on. What else did her ladyship say?" Richard was caught between amusement that Sadie would be such a minx and irritation that she thought to thwart his visit.

"Oh sir, I don't want to say."

"I won't hold you responsible for your lady's words."

"No, sir. She said she sends her regrets and that visiting hours are over, sir."

Richard paused. "Well, visiting hours are over. She is mistaken about a few other things, though. Where is she?"

"In the garden, sir."

"Thank you. Tina, is it?" The maid nodded. "Go on about your day. I'll respond to her message myself."

"Yes, Your Grace." Tina curtsied and quickly vanished.

Maybe it was time for another lesson for his lady.

Chapter 17 Time For Acceptance

Sadie was livid. He had left her to the mercy of his family. After all, Lady Margaret and Lady Julia were his mother and sister. They were very upset about having been left, as well. Was this what she was to expect when the man didn't want to face something? He would leave her to the wolves to save his own skin?

His mother and sister, while likely to tell him all that transpired, put Sadie on edge. She didn't know them, didn't understand how they thought or how they felt about the upcoming nuptials. When her friends had shown up, Sadie had forgotten they were coming for the final discussion on her dress, her breakfast, and just how she was dealing with her nerves. It was overwhelming and then, the rogue knave left her to her own devices.

Then, when Annalise mentioned how fortunate it was that Richard was enamored of Sadie, so that the ordeal of having a guardian over her property was unnecessary, Sadie shattered. Upon further inquiry, Lady Thayer stumbled over her words. Her stricken look told it all. Richard was to be her guardian, only to make it easier, he simply had chosen to marry her. Outrageous.

Sharing her feelings was difficult even with the ladies sometimes but absolutely impossible with her future mother-in-law. And now to learn that Richard was charged to look over her was insulting. Devastating.

After all of this, the man had the audacity to ask for an audience with her. No, let's be clear, he didn't ask for an audience, he summoned her. *Summoned her.* Sadie made another irritated stomp through the garden, watching the stone path to allow her to keep her footing when she slammed into a hard chest, and she knew who it was. His scent instantly surrounded her when she was forced to take notice.

"What else can you want from me today, sir?"

"Excuse me?"

Sadie tried to walk around Richard, and he corralled her with his arms, forestalling any attempts to leave his presence. "You are excused. Please step aside, sir. I am walking off my temper."

"Sarah, look at me."

She didn't. How could she when the fear she would say something unforgivable or worse, pushing him out of her way, out of her life, was real?

"Sarah. Look. At. Me. Immediately."

There was no quarter asked in his request or his expectation. She would have to comply and damn that she had to fight her own urge to do so which was at least equal to her anger. She determined she would give no quarter either. And this was her home. She had the right to deny anyone entrance. She had learned her lesson in that.

Sadie raised her head, and her eyes met his. Her stare was unwavering. "Your Grace, I am not in a proper state of mind to entertain you today. Please leave."

"And I might understand if I had the correct information but as you have not provided it, I feel honor bound to stay until you do."

Sadie looked at him as though she suddenly understood. "And that is the truth of it. Your honor. You are doing all of this because you feel honor bound. No matter your words to me, it is your obligation to take care of me that motivates you. Not out of commitment or because you believe I will be a good wife and mother, but because of your over-inflated duty. I don't wish to continue this farce, for even I was beginning to believe it. Shame on you, sir."

Richard gently held her arms, but Sadie knew without a doubt that she was going nowhere without his agreement. "Come inside, Sarah."

Not Sadie, but Sarah. He was serious. That was appropriate because so was she. Her problem was she wanted Richard to tell her Annalise had it all tangled. She'd misunderstood somehow, and he was going to straighten things out, but his response wasn't reassuring Sadie. It wasn't promising a clearer explanation.

The fight eked out of her very soul. She didn't want to talk to him, didn't want him to agree with her accusations. Didn't want to lose him.

"Richard, leave me with some dignity and just go."

"I will leave eventually, but your dignity is not something I can guarantee will remain unscathed. Nor a few other things that you obviously need more clarification on and attention to. Back to the library, milady, and not another word of dissent."

Now Richard was irate, and Sadie suppressed a shiver of anticipation. She didn't fear him, but she did wonder if he was angry because she had discovered him to be untruthful. He was likely cross because of her lack of trust in his motives. But if he looked at this situation from her perspective, how could she be anything but suspicious?

"Fine."

Sadie stepped out of his hold and stalked to the garden entrance and knew him to be directly behind her. Once inside, she sat in an armchair to keep her distance. Richard went to the sideboard and poured two whiskeys.

He set one cut-glass tumbler in front of Sadie who ignored it. Richard took a healthy taste from his glass and sat it on the end table.

"Now, you may begin to explain what you were talking about and why you came to such an utter nonsensical conclusion as I am marrying you out of duty. Mind your words, Sarah. It is important that you are respectful."

"Respectful. Yes, that is important to a duke who expects all will afford him that courtesy but what is your expected behavior towards others?"

"Sarah... mind how you go. When this is sorted out, you will be answering for your choices. Go easy, my love."

Sadie stalled with a moment of doubt. Did she misinterpret? No, Annalise was clear that Lord Henderson had asked Richard to be guardian over her until she married. But he called her my love. Not just a passing endearment to one you feel an obligation towards.

"Lord Henderson asked you to serve as my guardian until I married."

"That is correct. I received a letter from the solicitor, written by Lord Henderson, that requested I see to your protection until you marry, among other things. The follow-up letter he left with Mr. Shackleford should I go to him to inquire about further instructions also indicated that desire."

"And you chose to keep that to yourself."

"I did. It was an informal request, nothing set up with Shackleford, although he knew the contents of the letter and was prepared to create that guardianship if needed. He asked me if that was my desire, and I declined, in the hopes that what Lord Henderson and I had discussed prior to his death was going to be more permanent than that."

"Marriage." Richard nodded but said nothing.

"Why did you want to marry me? I'm not titled, I was educated well enough by Lady Henderson but not in any other way. I will embarrass you and any children we have. I'm not worthy of a man like you, with your wealth, estate, title, upbringing..." Sadie shrugged. "Therefore, it follows that it must be an obligation. There is no other reasonable explanation."

"There is no other one that you can think of? Because I am tired of answering this question. Once we have settled it today, I forbid you to question my motives again. Ever."

"Well, of course, there is affection, but how can that be more? I believe you love me in a friendship kind of way, but more than that? No, that isn't possible. You fool yourself and me if you think it is truly more."

"Then you have more to learn about love between a man and his wife than I had known. Sarah, I have not lied to you. Did I withhold the contents of Henderson's letter? I did, and this very reason is why. You believed it was my reason for reaching out to you. It was the stimulus that prompted my earlier return, but not the reason I want you as mine."

"Then why?"

"I've told you. Sarah, I have the strongest of affections towards you. I love you and have since you allowed me to offer, in jest, to chastise you for spying. Then when you set me down soundly in our walk around the parlor, I was never the same. Each correspondence assured me you were the one I wanted. You have allowed me to be the papa to your Darling when the occasion presents."

"But you have done everything a guardian would do. You saved me from the Flanders, put the house in order, watched over me, and introduced me to your friends, which is what a guardian would do."

"With the caveat that I did it because I wanted you. I had been inquiring of Lord Henderson for the last two years of his life if I could declare myself to you, but he declined. It was a concession he indicated was because of the mourning periods. It was more."

"But why did he speak of you to me in a complimentary way?"

"Because he wanted us to wed, he simply wanted to be selfish and keep you to himself. He had permitted me to tell you of my desires just before I came out of mourning for my father. He said it was time."

Sadie shook her head as though she couldn't completely comprehend the whole. "He was lonely."

"Yes, and you were young. Besides that, he knew what he was leaving you and wanted to safeguard you. However, I already knew that I wanted you and would have done whatever I needed to do to ensure you married me."

"I misjudged you."

"You most certainly misjudged me, and you will pay for it, but I prefer to wait until we are married. You will learn to trust your thinking in time. I will see to that. Sarah, be assured that my manhood that you gazed at during that evening at O'Leary's dinner table and that tingling that I make you feel right here." His hand touched her low on her belly. He listened to her sudden intake of breath and was slow to remove his touch. "That is the lust you feel for me. I feel the same. When you dream of me, do you imagine my touch on your skin? In your intimate places? Do you feel desperate to discover that reality? That is what we have between us. Need and want, ache and desire comes from that love we have nurtured between us these years. Accept that there is this and so much more that I want to give you and that I want from you.

"I was so afraid that my trust was once again misplaced, but it tore at my heart, for I have the deepest of affections towards you as well, my Grace. I don't know how to stop those thoughts of being inferior."

"I will teach you that you are perfect for me."

He stood and crossed to her. He leaned down to kiss the top of her head, and Sadie leaned heavily into the arms he slid over her shoulders and then sat back in his wide chair.

"I wish I knew the date so we can get this over with."

Richard leaned over and grabbed Sadie's hand and tugged to encourage her to come to him. He opened his arms when she stood in front of him and when she crawled into his lap, he wrapped around her, placing his head on her shoulder.

"This is improper, sir," Sadie said as she snuggled in closer.

Richard nodded. "It is. But so was riding in my carriage without an escort, staying in my house without another female family member present, calling each other by our given names in private, and I imagine many more things, but that will soon be over."

"But when? I do not believe the duchess or your sister wants me to become part of your family. I'm not what they expected you to be happy with."

"Sarah, did they tell you that?" His voice was deceptively calm, but she could hear his tone alert.

"No, but when I would offer them more refreshments or to help plan the particulars of the wedding breakfast afterward, they declined. They both said it was nice to meet me but not that we should further the acquaintance or come for luncheon or anything. And now I am duty bound to return the visit."

Richard chuckled as Sadie bemoaned her plight. "Shh, my dear. I promise to stay at the next meeting, which will be tonight. I wish for you to have dinner, and we will settle the matter once and for all. Our wedding date is a week from tomorrow."

Sadie was at once excited and apprehensive. "I need to send a message to the ladies."

"Do not bother with messages. I have delivered a personal invitation for all to join us for dinner this evening. One announcement will suffice."

Richard discussed his errands as she told him of her morning. He promised to have a serious conversation with his sister and mother and make sure that there was no misunderstanding about their upcoming wedding. It was going to happen. Sadie felt better; however, she still had some genuine concerns about the outcome. What if they didn't agree to accept his choice? Would that make him change his mind?

"Sarah, what are you thinking so hard about?"

"What if they don't agree?"

"About the wedding? Then they do not need to bother coming," Richard answered as he rubbed her back.

"But it will be most unpleasant if your family doesn't like me or agree with your wedding."

"What must I say or do to convince you that I have fallen totally and completely in love with the woman who will be my Darling Duchess?"

Sadie sighed. "Nothing, my duke. Nothing at all."

Chapter 18 Time For A New Mistress

Marriage was a very serious business to many people, so Sadie discovered when the official announcement was penned, ready to put into the society papers the moment the deed was done. Word was out that Richard Gerald Griffin, the Duke of Amesbury, was going to be wed to an unknown. Lady Julia and Lady Margaret were a significant source of entertainment in their animation of the details they heard when visiting old friends.

Both women had changed their tune when they saw how many people were talking about how daring a move it was and so like the duke to take a risk and make it good. And after her duke had a conversation with the women in his family about his expectations, there was never a skewed glance between them. Sadie relaxed. Richard could be quite stern when the occasion called for it.

"Sarah, you will not believe how popular you have become with Londoners," said Lady Margaret.

Sarah sat on the sofa in her house with an enormous sigh. "Yes, so I understand, but I don't want to be the talk of anyone. That is why everyone is filling my door and leaving their cards, I imagine. They practically sell tickets like I am a sideshow. Your Grace says not to entertain them, but how can I not?"

"He is quite right, though," said Lady Margaret. "I do like the attention for Julia's sake, but you must not stress yourself over something like this right before you stand before the Bishop."

Julia grinned. "When I am ready to marry, I will make sure we have the banns read as well to ensure that I have many callers. Otherwise, marriage is so anticlimactic, don't you think?"

"You may have mine if you like. Did you know what one woman had the audacity to say to me? She said in plain words that the Duke of Amesbury wasn't called the Daring Duke for naught."

Julia sniffed. "That is impressively rude and familiar. I wish Richard were given to allow gossip. It is taking the enjoyment out of these encounters. I could have just great enjoyment in creating stories to start tongues wagging."

"The cheek of the woman," said Sadie.

"This is the last day, my dear. Tomorrow you will stand up with Richard and that will be the end of that."

"I suppose. That is what Rosemary has said but I'm not sure."

"Well, she is considered more American than British, so I can see as she quite understands being an oddity."

"Why would women who claim an attachment to your family think that gives them the right to call on me?"

"I don't believe they do, but you know that women who are trying to produce an alliance will do bold things."

"But I do not want to discuss anything of a personal nature with women who suddenly demand an audience." Even if that audience was never more than fifteen minutes.

"I am well and truly too busy to entertain many of the gawkers. Besides, Richard has plenty of demands on my time, as it is."

The duchess agreed. "I saw he required your input on things pertaining to business. That is not done. You have the household to keep you busy. Women should not be as hard at work as men. Our temperaments lend us to more docile engagements in the day."

"I enjoy working the accounts or deciding on the duke's next adventure. I appreciate you sacrificing your mornings to help me receive these women."

Lady Margaret and Lady Thayer were both very adept at keeping the comments and questions reasonable. No one pressed those ladies. They were quite severe if crossed.

Richard insisted on a dinner with friends and family the evening before the nuptials and a wedding breakfast after. He insisted on Saint George's Hanover Square, and he insisted on the Bishop presiding. There was the expectation that she wear a dress she had never worn before, but she was free to wear it after the wedding. She was to share her room and bed with him on the wedding night, and he insisted that she discuss things with the ladies about what that night might look like.

Her challenge of such things with Richard was first met with a laugh and dismissal that it was what one did.

"One expects to be with your spouse on your wedding night."

"It isn't that I deny that time with you, Your Grace. It is that I do not want to discuss such intimacies with anyone. Not even you, nor do I intend to do so."

Her pouts of resistance and the stamping of her foot did not enhance his mood, however, and landed her prostrate over his desk two days before the wedding.

"I am not ready to follow your mandates my whole life, Your Grace."

"No? Well, you had better come with a good reason if you will challenge me. I am happy to leave you the running of the household and staff, except Mr. Arnold and my personal people, but if I say it is to be done, you will not question me. I would only ever issue a mandate if it were vital for your safety and happiness."

"Sir, can you not ask me?"

"Usually, yes, but not when there is no freedom of choice available. And that happens occasionally. These things concerning the wedding are not negotiable."

"I cannot discuss such things as marital subjects. Not with you and not with another woman. I will be mortified and deemed inappropriate. It isn't done, sir."

"Sarah, I am not in the mood to argue about everything that must happen."

"Then don't force me to do all these things that have little use. I mean, husbands do not share rooms with their wives."

"They do at least part of the night and often all the night."

"They do not. I have lived in the house with Lord and Lady Henderson, and they kept their own bed chambers and slept in their own beds."

"How do you know?"

"Because they went to bed at different times. She was often in bed before he went up."

Richard grabbed Sadie by the hand and brought her into Lord Henderson's room, officially his in a few days. He had most of his things in the suite of chambers now, but he still had the ceremony to prepare for so those things and his toiletries were at the townhouse that his mother and sister would stay in, along with all the staff they brought from Amesbury House.

"Where do you think this door goes to?"

Sarah shrugged elegantly. His beautiful Sarah was becoming more confident and sassier. "His dressing room or sitting room, I imagine."

"Open it."

"Richard, I'm not in the mood to go through this room. I have a dinner party and a formal breakfast to prepare to oversee."

"Do it, Sarah." His tone brooked no argument, and Sadie had learned when to stop pushing back.

She opened the door. "See, to his dressing room and sitting room."

"And where does that door in the corner open to?"

"I do not know. Likely a passageway."

But she was beginning to get an idea. Sadie approached the door and had a flashback of the evening when she overheard her benefactor's conversation. A papa and a Darling. Lord and Lady Henderson. And it had never dawned on her that the door she heard shut must have taken him to another room, but where?

She opened the door and peered into the entry. It opened into Lady Henderson's dressing room and sitting room, which led into the bedchamber. "I never knew," Sadie whispered. "I heard things but never thought it was Lord Henderson entering her room."

"Have the conversation with your ladies, Sarah. You will be happy you did. After breakfast, I plan to take the men to shoot, and mother and Julia plan to go back to the townhouse. That would be the perfect time to discuss the evening activities."

"Can I not just learn as things, um, happen?"

"Sadie, papa said to stop your protesting. It is the established way, and this is not a place where one should break with tradition. Now, come look at the jewels I have brought with me and choose your ring and other jewelry for our special day."

THE WEDDING REVELRY began at six p.m. and Sadie was already feeling the strain of the event. Worry lingered that her duke would not want her as his wife after the initial novelty had worn off. She didn't have what it took to be his wife. Or rather, she had too much to learn to be the wife he needed.

But sitting in the corner of the grand parlor, watching her strong, protective man still hosting, still entertaining, still going strong at midnight told her he was vibrant, engaged in this adventure and he was ready for the next stage of his life. And when he would catch her eye, his became intense with a heat she was becoming familiar with, but not what it offered her. He assured her their first night would make the fullness of that gift abundantly clear.

After the wedding, she was to discuss things pertaining to that time with her friends. The wives of the duke's friends. It was daunting. As daunting as the anticipation of that night itself. Sadie looked up and saw her view was blocked by someone and that person's presence spoke to her soul long before she could inhale his scent or observe his clothing or face. Sadie smiled.

This man.

"Are you well, princess?" He asked her discreetly.

"I am. I am tired and ready for my bed, Your Grace, but sitting here affords me a good view of the festivities without having to fully participate. Do you think badly of me? That I am avoiding those who are happy for us?"

He defied convention to squat down, even in his tight breeches, to look into her eyes and give her comfort. Did any woman's man do such things for their woman? Possibly, but this was the only man she had eyes for.

"Shall I take you to your room? Make your excuses? Tomorrow will be a long day, and the next few days will be taxing as well. I intend to tire my wife out during her first days as my duchess."

His meaning was clear, now that she knew a little more of the marriage bed and the desires of her duke's heart. Maybe she should ask the ladies, very discreetly, of course. She shook her head.

"I am fading, it is true, but I can stay longer to appreciate the gaiety. Do not worry about me. I shall do fine."

Earlier, Sadie had been so distressed that all the preparations were not to standard, that Richard had encouraged her to have a brandy, and when she would have refused, he offered her mead instead. She liked honey wine and before he could stop her, she'd had three glasses.

"That will be quite enough of that wine, my dear." She pouted prettily and Richard leaned down to share his thoughts privately. "I love you so much my dear but that doesn't extend to allowing you to have whatever you desire if it is to your detriment. You will be in your cups soon. That is not the impression you want to leave in people's memory of your wedding."

"I do feel a little dizzy, Richard. I think I will be sick."

He had rushed her to the garden and let her toss the majority of the wine and the entire contents of her stomach next to the potter's shack. He grabbed the shovel left there and tossed some dirt over the leavings and walked her in the crisp March evening air.

"Better?"

"Yes, so much better. That has never happened to me before."

"I have never allowed you three glasses in such a short time before. I am now warned and will not do so again. Two within several hours is all you may have. I would that you remember this lesson when I restrict your intake next time, my princess."

"I thought you would be angry."

"No, I know where the need to look for Dutch courage came from, but be on notice, rely on me to lessen your distress, not wine. The outcome will be better, I promise."

He leaned down to kiss her lips, and she turned away with her hand over her mouth.

"Please do not, sir. My mouth. I just..."

He laughed and kissed the corner of her mouth. "You soon find that a man in love with a woman doesn't care how she looks or the scent of her. It is she that he wants. So do not expect that I won't take you before a bath or after a long day of travel, for that will not deter me from devouring your luscious body." He walked her inside. "Go rinse your mouth, my love, for I will want your lips before you sleep tonight."

Richard looked at his Darling Duchess now as she sat stiffly in an uncomfortable chair and debated whether he would give her a few more moments of the party or whisk her away immediately to bed. She looked exhausted, and to leave her here worked hard against every bit of his protectiveness, but he pushed past it.

Just for a few more minutes. He kissed her hand when he wanted her sweet lips, for to break with convention at this hour would have scandalized his mother and serve a precedent he did not want to set for Julia. This would be the last evening he would go to bed without his princess.

Richard found her in the same corner of the room, sitting up, as he had left her fifteen minutes ago, now fast asleep. He left the celebrants and put his princess to bed alone for the very last time, leaving her with kissed lips as he had promised.

THE WEDDING SEEMED to go on forever, but now they were at the book signing and all would be official in less than a minute. So many words she couldn't remember half of, the family ring she wore on her finger and the promise ring Richard had given her, lay on the finger beside it. The two rings fought for dominance on one finger, and while her new mother-in-law suggested removing the betrothal ring, she declined.

Richard had given them both to her and she would wear them both, for now at least. Maybe wearing it on the opposite hand after a time would be more comfortable, but for now, she wanted to have them both. The statement of ruby, diamonds, and emeralds was impressive.

They represented a long road to arrive at today. Sadie thought of those loved ones that got her to this place and knew life had gifted her with more than anyone would have thought on the day of her birth. Looking at Lord Richard Griffin, the Duke of Amesbury as he conversed quietly with the other witnesses and guests, as the clerk and the Bishop signed the last places on the page, Sadie had a moment of doubt. Did he truly love her, or did he marry her because he was the Daring Duke and it was his penchant to take those endeavors with low prospects and bring them to greater heights?

Then she looked into his face as he peered into hers. No, this man loved her, maybe more than she loved him. It had been hard getting to know him with so many conventions and social barriers in place. It had been hard learning about love, about Richard, and finding a place where her love and her desperate need for autonomy didn't collide into a roaring fire. It still would, occasionally, but knowing her duke loved her and that no matter what transpired, he would be there to hold her, kiss her, and chastise her, gave her a calm that she had not felt in a very long time.

"Come my love. We are leaving now. Everyone will meet us at Dwyer. Your dress is the perfect shade of blue to make your eyes sparkle. It is glorious to behold. You make a beautiful bride, my love."

"You flatter me."

"Soon, I will do more than that."

The thrill that made her body tremble was overwhelming, and at that moment, whatever he had planned for them later was something she wanted more than anything. Wanted it now.

"I know, my love. I know. Soon you will speak to your friends, and then you will be ready for me. Know I will be gentle and careful."

Sadie did not know what he was talking about other than what one could glean in life. But she was ready.

Chapter 19 Time To Begin Forever

The moment he informed the butler, Mr. Carrier, that he and Sadie were going to Henderson House and would return the next afternoon, was the moment he had been waiting for since he saw her in the foyer that night they were formally introduced.

Taking her hand, he left her to Quillie, who had turned into a decent maid under the careful training of Mrs. Arnold, who loved Sadie like her own mother. Like Lady Henderson.

Evidently, the house had been waiting for them and the moment the carriage pulled up, the house went into action. Fires in the bedroom he was to occupy, Henderson's room before him. It was large, and the bed roomy. The room was sweet-smelling with a spiciness not meant for sleep. Richard smiled. There was not much left to chance. The bath was being drawn as he entered and he expected his princess... no, his *duchess* was likely experiencing the same treatment.

When he was relaxed and thoroughly clean, he sent his valet to have Mrs. Arnold finish Sadie's bath and send him word when she was ready to dress. Richard didn't want Sarah to worry about any awkwardness or pleasing him. He would rather simply take her by surprise. Evidently, Mrs. Arnold agreed, for she didn't try to dissuade him.

Walking through the connecting door, Richard gazed on Sadie as she stood from the bath.

"Quillie, I am finished with my bath."

He grabbed the flannel sheet left for her to dry with and came up behind her. As he wrapped the cloth around her, she stepped from the bath. Wrapping her completely in the material, he kissed her neck. She stiffened and then, as he continued to kiss her exposed shoulder and neck, Sarah spoke.

"You are not Quillie. My husband may not be very happy to know his new wife is being ravaged by another before he has had his fill."

"Mmm, bold words from a woman who has no idea what she is about to experience."

"She has an idea, sir."

"Does she indeed? Then let me educate her further."

His kisses became heated, his hands pushed the fabric away to make way for his hands as they caressed her breasts. Such beautiful, full breasts. The gowns gave no indication of the lushness of her endowments. She smelled so sweet his body ached for the intensity.

"I love you, my duchess. Let me love you with my body."

Her answering moan was all he needed to take her to paradise. While she still stood near the bath, her body drying in the heat of the crackling fire, he swooped her up to stand near the bed, awash with firelight and a few candles nearest the bed on the side tables.

"It's beautiful in here, Richard. More enchanting than I have ever seen it."

"You are beautiful, enchanting, and the elements are trying to match your glory. They have far to go."

His tongue touched her nipple and she cried out. The little bit of flesh ruched and puckered and her breath hitched. His cock jumped in answer to her body's responses. And so it went, his mouth covered hers, his tongue explored her warm depths and she reached to hold him, grasp him as though he were her lifeline. Indeed he was.

He played with her breasts, her nipples were hard, pointy, and needy. His cock was the same. He slid his hand down past a flat belly that would soon be swollen with his child and his urgency increased. She was his and he needed to take possession.

Gentle, he reminded himself and as his hand eased down her belly, followed by his kisses, he touched her intimately. More intimately than her mouth, her breasts, her belly. He slid his fingers past her downy guard to her prize, her core. His mouth followed.

"No, Richard, you must not."

"I can do no other, my sweet duchess. You are so hot, wet, and slippery with your need for me. I am hard with my need for you. This is what you have been in need of, the final bit of me that I am giving to you, freely, reverently, eagerly."

While he spoke to her, he had found her little button of excitement. He gently circled and rubbed. She gushed, and he groaned his need.

"Please..."

"I know, my sweet. A little more."

"It's too much... too much."

She stiffened, froze into place, and then she sat up in the overcoming power of her orgasm. He brought her to the heights of her need and like the crashing of the cymbals, the waves against a craggy coast, she screamed in her first experience of ecstasy.

Richard quickly slipped further down and lapped at her now deep red intimate areas and put his tongue into her sheath. She cried out again, the perspiration covering her skin, he licked her inner thigh, it was salty and heated with her perfume.

Kissing and sucking was not enough now, his cock was about to explode and he had been working on his endurance but there were limits to his abilities. As she was still in the throes of her second climax, he circled his cockhead with her juices, running it up and down her reactive pussy. He watched her face as she began to relax, it was time.

Richard slipped his cock into her sheath and the pressure from untried tissue had untried muscles clamp and resist his entrance. Sadie's eyes opened.

"Sir?"

"Shush my sweet, I will be gentle as I can."

He teased her nipples as he gritted his teeth in restraint. She felt incredible on just the head of his cock, the total immersion would be divine. He kissed her lips and ran his hands lightly over her skin, bringing his kiss to her nips and his finger to her intimate button. Richard could feel her tighten again and he feared she would expel him. He held her tightly, God in heaven she was so perfect. She reached out and clasped his forearms. He felt her dam break with another rush of ecstasy and he slid steadily past the barrier, past the tight muscles, and seated fully in her sheath. Home.

After a moment's recovery, he smiled when Sarah said, "I'm ready."

"Ready for what, my love, I am fully seated, I have but to move but I am fully engaged. We are one being."

She lay as though to take in his words and then she sighed. "So we are. It was not so dramatic as I had feared."

Richard chuckled and tweaked a nipple. "I am not done yet."

SHE WAS HOT AND SWEATY but no more than he. Richard watched as the sun came up on their second day of wedded bliss. He did not know that what he wanted her to learn about before the wedding bed would be much more powerful with the woman you loved. Richard looked over at his sleeping wife. Sarah was more than he had ever imagined. Richard lay in bed and thought about the last couple of days.

The ups and downs and the last-minute fears that he had to push away. Now they were married. None of the worries that she would leave, hide from him, push him away before this moment was gone. Sarah was the only woman he had ever been concerned would reject him. She had not. And the life they would lead would be rich and full.

"Do you think I am with child?"

Richard kissed her. "We have had congress only three times, my love. I believe it will take more than that."

"Oh? Are you an expert?"

"No, and no we are not engaging in more of the same until you have soaked the aches away, we have had some nourishment, and you have rejuvenated some."

"I am a bit sore, but you are adept at working out the aches." Sarah reached out to him and touched his stiff cock. "And it appears I am not the only one with that opinion."

"Sarah, I have said no."

"Hmm, yes, Your Grace." Her hand slid up and down his cock in a firm, then tender grip.

Richard groaned and rolled over. He crushed her lips whispering against them, "Minx. I should spank your naughty arse."

"Yes, Your Grace."

The End

About the Author
Alyssa Bailey

USA Today and #1 Bestselling Author of Diverse Romance that is realistic and sensual with a touch of suspense. A dyed in the wool Texan living in Alaska for half her life, Alyssa now divides her time between the beauty of Southeast Alaska and the piney woods of East Texas. She enjoys taking from her own experiences to create series in fictitious worlds to tease the reader's palate and invite them to sink into exciting adventures.

Alyssa enjoys writing consensual power exchanges between intelligent, sassy women who are not afraid to make a stand and loving men confident enough to give his woman space but masterful enough to keep her safe despite her choices. There is *always* a happily ever after.

Follow me on Goodreads:
https://www.goodreads.com/author/show/14149220.Alyssa_Bailey
Visit me online and sign up for my Newsletter:
http://alyssabailey.com[1]
Join my Facebook Group for fun and prizes:
https://www.facebook.com/alyssabailey.romance
Find me on Social Media:
https://linktr.ee/alyssabailey

---

1. http://alyssabailey.com/

More Alyssa Bailey Romances

Lords and Little Ladies: Regency Historical, Spicy
    Lord Thayer's Choice
Lord Ashton's Decision
The Black Laird Requires
Lord Kendrick's Obligation

DARLING DUCHESSES: Regency, Daddy Dom, Spicy
<u>Devil Duke's Little Distraction (Book 1)</u>[1]
Chase Abbey Series: Regency, Spicy, Suspense
Lord Barrington's Minx
Becoming Lady Barrington
Lady Caroline's Defiance
His Improper Lady

SAFE AND SECURE SERIES: Contemporary, Suspense, Spicy
Saving Sharlee
Saving Jessie
Saving Ivy
Securing Mallory
Securing Callie
Securing Becky (2023)
Securing Finley (2023)

---

1.   https://books2read.com/TheDevilDuke

THE O'CONNORS: THE Complete Collection
The O'Connor Series: Contemporary, Rancher, DD, Spicy
Liam & Jocelyn's Story
Her Sweet Complication
Liam's Lessons
Loving Liam

CIARÁN AND KATHERINE'S Story
His Gentle Persuasion
Rancher's Creed
Katie Consents

QUINLAN AND CHEYENNE'S Story
Quinlan's Quest
Accepting His Way
Her Balancing Act

KELLI AND PARKER'S Story
Meeting Her Needs
Kissing Kelli
Keeping Kelli

CIÁN AND MOLLY'S STORY
In Pursuit of Molly
Freeing Molly
Forever Molly

LONE WIND SERIES: Contemporary, Spicy, Native American

Reclaiming Clover

CLEARWATER RANCH TRILOGY -Contemporary, Spicy, Alpha
Piper's Plan
Camille's Second Chance
Josie's Refuge

TAMING TEXANNA-American Historical, Native American, Spicy
Cowboy Welcome- Contemporary, Spicy
In the Spirit of Christmas -Contemporary, Sweet

RED EAGLE RANCH- Contemporary, Rancher, Spicy, Multi-Cultural
Stryker's Girl (Book 1)
Declan's Girl (Book 2)
Seamus' Girl (Book 3)
Jacob's Girl (Book 4) (2023)
Callen's Girl (Book 5) (2023)
Renee's Reward (Book 6) (2023)

GUARDIANS OF REFUGE- Contemporary, Military, Spicy
SEAL of Refuge (Book 1)
The Strategy of Love (Book 2)
The Tactics of Love (Book 3)
The Mandate of Love (Book 4)

SAGE COUNTY
Deep Waters (Book 1)
Still Waters (Book 2)

STATESIDE DOMS (ASSORTED authors-Heat Varies)
Stateside Doms- Her Wyoming Dream Daddy

ANTHOLOGIES (HEAT VARIES)
Sweet Town Love
Historical Heroes
Dirty Discipline-Volume 2 (Dirty Discipline Duet)

MULTI-AUTHOR BOX SETS (Heat Level Various)
Love, Christmas 2 Recipes
FREE Book Bites 11
FREE Book Bites 13
Irresistible Heroes
Tempting Protectors
Sweet and Sassy Summertime Vol. 2
Dear Santa: A Christmas Wish
Sweet and Sassy New Beginnings

Don't miss out!

Visit the website below and you can sign up to receive emails whenever Alyssa Bailey publishes a new book. There's no charge and no obligation.

https://books2read.com/r/B-A-MXIL-MPBGC

BOOKS 2 READ

Connecting independent readers to independent writers.

Did you love *The Daring Dukes Little Impulse*? Then you should read *The Devil Duke's Distraction* by Alyssa Bailey!

Falling in love was never part of the bargain.

Lady Sofia Cloverfield's family has disintegrated, and she finds herself on the streets to make her own way with only a few guineas and her wits with which to rely on to survive. Sofia uses her common sense and prays she can figure out how to turn her fate around.

Exeter Trenton, the Devil Duke, is wealthy, handsome, and lonely. His position demands he take a wife, but he finds none to his liking. Then, quite by accident, his luck changes when his horses nearly trample a waif he mistakes for a child. He allows her to leave with his chastisement ringing in her ear but not before he finds she is no child.

Once home, Trenton finds he can't get the little minx out of his mind. Telling himself he would be creating a better life for her, he devises a plan to bring her home for a brief distraction.

The Duke initially intends to enjoy her attributes and teach her the thrills of being a woman with an attentive lover. One who engages in incomparable pleasures while remaining diligent in keeping her safe, but plans change, and before he can stop her, his little distraction has gotten under his skin and crawled into his heart.

Now the Devil Duke can never let her go.

Just as Sofia realizes Trenton is more dangerous than she ever suspected, her heart is engaged, and her life is at risk, forcing her to draw on every skill she has learned to save herself from a fate she had barely escaped several times before.

The Duke's goals for Sofia may have changed, but not even the confident, masterful, and influential Duke can see into the future and know that someone else has a different ending planned for his Fia... a very different ending.

Read more at alyssabailey.com.

Also by Alyssa Bailey

Darling Duchesses
The Daring Dukes Little Impulse

Watch for more at alyssabailey.com.

www.ingramcontent.com/pod-product-compliance
Lightning Source LLC
Chambersburg PA
CBHW030255270626
47156CB00022B/2765